MARY ANNE AND THE MUSIC BOX SECRET

MARY ANNE AND THE
MUSIC BOX SECRET

Ann M. Martin

AN
APPLE
PAPERBACK

SCHOLASTIC INC.
New York Toronto London Auckland Sydney

Cover art by Hodges Soileau

ISBN 0-590-69179-1

12 11 10 9 8 7 6 5 4 3 2 1   7 8 9/9 0 1 2/0

Printed in the U.S.A.   40
First Scholastic printing, August 1997

The author gratefully acknowledges
Ellen Miles
for her help in
preparing this manuscript.

CHAPTER 1

"**W**here are they? How can they possibly have disappeared overnight?" I heard Sharon asking herself questions as she rushed from room to room. "Mary Anne," she called, finally, "have you seen my — "

"Car keys?" I asked, holding them up as she hurried into the kitchen to meet me. "They were in the bread box," I said, smiling.

Sharon smiled back ruefully as she accepted the keys. "Why didn't I save myself time and just look there in the first place?" she asked.

"If you had, they wouldn't have been there," said my father, from behind the newspaper. "They would have been in the bathroom cabinet or in your underwear drawer." He gave a little snort and peered over the paper. "The one place we know they'd never be in is on the key rack." Dad shook his head and grinned. He'd brought home that key rack one evening and hung it on the wall near the back door. Every

1

single day, when he comes home from work, he hangs his keys on the hook marked RICHARD. But the hook marked SHARON is always empty. Which isn't a surprise to anyone who knows Sharon. And my dad doesn't really seem to mind. He's become accustomed to Sharon's ways, just as she's become accustomed to his. (Though I'm sure she freaked out the first time she saw him alphabetizing the cans of Campbell's soup in our cabinet.)

Sharon is my stepmother, and I love her dearly even though she is, to put it politely, organizationally challenged. In case you're wondering, I take after my dad when it comes to liking things neat and tidy. But I've learned to accept and even enjoy Sharon's less structured approach to life.

My name is Mary Anne Spier, and I'm thirteen years old. I have brown hair and brown eyes, and I'm a little short for my age. I'm in the eighth grade at Stoneybrook Middle School (which is in Stoneybrook, Connecticut), but at the moment I'm enjoying those lazy, crazy days of summer vacation. August is a great month, isn't it? Everybody's relaxed and happy. You live in shorts, sandals, and a T-shirt, with occasional changes into a bathing suit. School seems a long way off. Aaaah, August!

Sharon and my dad don't necessarily share my feelings about August. That's because they still have to work. My dad is a lawyer, and Sharon is a realtor. I work, too; I do a lot of baby-sitting and even belong to this great club called the BSC, the Baby-sitters Club. (More about that later.) But it's not as if I work full-time.

That August Thursday, Sharon and Dad had both taken the day off. Why? Because we had a big family event to attend. Sharon's parents (I call them Granny and Pop-Pop even though they're my stepgrands) were about to set off on a special anniversary cruise, and we were all headed down to the dock in New York City to see their ship off.

All of us who were in Stoneybrook, that is. I wished Dawn could be with us. That's Dawn Schafer, Sharon's daughter and my stepsister. She lives in California.

Confused? I don't blame you. My family situation is complicated. Let me explain.

First of all, my mom died when I was very, very young. I never even knew her. My dad was devastated at the time and couldn't deal with raising an infant daughter, so he sent me away — temporarily — to live with my grandparents in Iowa. After awhile, when he'd worked through the worst of his grief, he sent for me, but my grandparents didn't want to give me up. Finally, after a custody struggle, my dad won me back.

I didn't know anything about my Iowa grandparents until recently. I was shocked when I found out.

Now I'm in touch with my grandmother in Iowa, and I've even visited her there. (My grandfather died before we could be reunited. I don't remember him at all.)

Anyway, back in Stoneybrook, my dad was trying hard to be both father and mother to me. He took parenting very seriously — *too* seriously, to tell you the truth. He made a lot of rules about what I could and couldn't do (for example, he wouldn't let me decorate my room with posters I chose) and what I could and couldn't wear (I was still in kiddie jumpers and braids when I was twelve). I'm not the most assertive person, so it took me awhile to realize that I should stand up to my dad. My best friend, Kristy Thomas, who may just be the most assertive person in the universe, helped me figure out how to do it. Eventually, I convinced him to treat me a little more like an adult.

Meanwhile, I had become a member of the BSC. And I had met Dawn, who had just moved to Stoneybrook from Palo City, California. While she had arrived from the West Coast, her roots are actually in Stoneybrook. Her mom, Sharon, grew up here, then moved out to California for college. She got married there, too. The marriage ended in divorce, so Mrs. Schafer brought her kids — Dawn and her younger brother, Jeff — back to Stoneybrook to live. Dawn and I became immediate best friends, and she ended up joining the BSC as well. Then one day we made an awesome discovery. While we were paging through some old Stoneybrook High yearbooks, we found out that our parents had *dated*, back when they were in high school.

We did some plotting and planning, and before you could say "old flames never die out," Sharon and my dad were an item again. Isn't that the most romantic story you ever heard? Sigh.

Anyway, not long after that, they decided to marry, and my dad and I moved into this cool old farmhouse (it even has a secret passage) with Sharon and Dawn. By that time, Jeff had come to realize that he was never going to feel at home on the East Coast, and he'd gone back to California to live with his dad. The rest of us took some time to adjust to one another — for awhile it was like a war between the Neatniks and the Slobs — but eventually we learned how to coexist pretty happily. That includes Sharon and my adorable gray tiger-striped kitten, Tigger. Sharon is not exactly a cat person, but she's learned at least to tolerate him.

We even came to enjoy each other's taste in

food, to an extent. Sharon and Dawn are into health food. They love nothing better than a plate of rice, beans, and veggies. My dad and I, meanwhile, are basically the meat-and-potatoes type. And while it's true that Sharon isn't about to dig into any T-bones, and my dad won't knowingly eat tofu (Sharon sneaks it into the occasional casserole), we have come to understand and even appreciate each other's preferences.

Once we ironed everything out, we were happy together. Or at least, that's what I thought. It turned out that Dawn was wrestling with some strong feelings. She missed California — her dad, her friends, and the place itself — all the time, even though she'd been going there regularly for vacations. Eventually, she made a huge decision. She wanted to move back there.

I can't say I wasn't hurt. I was. I was devastated, to tell you the truth. But I also tried hard to see things from Dawn's point of view. My friends say that's what I'm best at. They can't believe how sensitive I am, and they're always telling me I'm a great listener. To me it just comes naturally.

Anyway, I now understand that Dawn made the right decision — the only decision, for her. Still, I miss her very much. It's hard to lose a best friend *and* a sister all at once. But I do see her when she comes back for vacations. She was here earlier this summer, and we had a blast. (We had an even bigger blast when the BSC members drove Dawn back home. It was a road trip that will go down in history. But that's another story.)

So, now you know it all. Or most of it, anyway. I haven't told you about Logan Bruno, my adorable boyfriend with the sweet Southern accent (he moved here from Louisville, Kentucky), or about the ghost that may haunt the secret passage at my house, or about my friends in the BSC.

Still, you know enough to understand who I am and how my current family came to be. And I want to make it clear how much I love that current family. I may not have known Granny and Pop-Pop for very long, but they treat me like a granddaughter and I think of them as my grandparents. I was so happy for them that day. I knew they'd have a terrific time on their cruise.

Also, I knew something they *didn't* know: When they came back, they were going to be surprised with the best anniversary party anyone's ever had. Sharon had been planning it for months.

You might think Sharon wouldn't be so great at planning a big party, but you'd be surprised. She may be disorganized on a daily basis, but when it comes to major projects she knows how to pull them together. She keeps files and lists and notebooks full of names and numbers, and somehow she manages to keep track of every detail. When it really matters, Sharon is on the ball.

"Remember, now," Sharon said to me and my dad as we drove over to Granny and Pop-Pop's to pick them up for the ride to the ship. "If either of you breathes a *word* about the party I'll cover you with honey and tie you to an ant-hill."

I cracked up. Sharon is such a warm, gentle person. Threats like that sound absurd coming from her. "You don't have to worry," I promised. "My lips are sealed. What about Esther and Hank? Did you warn them, too?" Esther and Hank are Granny and Pop-Pop's best friends. Granny and Hank grew up in the same neighborhood, so they've known each other forever. He has always seemed like a grouch to me, but Esther is very nice.

"You bet," she said. "I told them I'd boil them in oil if they spilled the secret." She smiled sweetly.

"Boiling in oil just might improve Hank's disposition," muttered my dad. I'm not the only one who thinks Hank is grouchy.

Okay, fast forward to a huge dock in Manhattan. (Well, actually, the dock is in the Hudson River. But you know what I mean.) Now picture the biggest boat you've ever seen. And multiply that by a hundred. That's the ship Granny and Pop-Pop had booked their trip on. We'd had the grand tour of the many decks and pools, the elegant rooms, the movie theater, the library, and the health club. And we'd seen the tiny but charming stateroom, complete with porthole, that Granny and Pop-Pop would be living in for the next two weeks. All through the tour, Hank had been grumbling. "Too fancy for my blood," he commented, looking at a sample menu. "All right if you like that kind of thing," he'd said about the gym. And, finally, about the porthole, he'd remarked that "a window that size doesn't give you much of a view, does it, now?" Esther had shushed him, but Granny and Pop-Pop just laughed. They're used to Hank.

Finally, after a round of hugs, we left the ship and stood on the dock to watch as the crew made ready to sail. Granny and Pop-Pop leaned over the railing, throwing confetti and waving, along with all the other happy passengers. We waved back and kept on waving until the huge ship finally pulled away and we could hardly see Granny and Pop-Pop anymore.

"They're going to have a wonderful time," said Sharon, wiping a tear from her eye. I was feeling a little emotional, too. Seeing people off can do that to me. I don't know why.

"No question about it," said my dad. "They'll be happy as clams."

"As long as they don't run into any hurricanes," Hank said gloomily.

The rest of us just laughed. Hank was such a pessimist. What could possibly happen to ruin Granny and Pop-Pop's anniversary cruise?

CHAPTER 2

By the time our BSC meeting rolled around the next day, I was still thinking about that huge cruise ship. My friends and I once spent some time on a ship, but it wasn't nearly as big as the one Granny and Pop-Pop were on. I wondered how it would feel to be a passenger on a ship like that, and before I knew it I'd begun to fantasize about what it would be like to *work* on a cruise ship. Wouldn't that be awesome? Just think of it. What a way to earn a living! Sun and fun every day. Great meals. Exotic ports to visit. I could just picture the BSC members ten years from now, working our way around the world on an enormous ocean liner.

Before I become too carried away, I guess I should explain a little more about the BSC. Basically, we're a group of responsible, experienced baby-sitters who meet three times a week: Monday, Wednesday, and Friday afternoons, from five-thirty until six. During those

11

times, parents can call to set up sitting jobs. When they use the BSC, parents know they're hiring sitters they can count on, sitters who love kids. We have a great time with our charges, whether we're doing an organized activity or just hanging out. Sometimes, especially on rainy days, we bring along our Kid-Kits: boxes we've filled with stickers, markers, and hand-me-down toys, books, and games.

We keep a club notebook in which each of us records every job we go on (parents love the fact that we're always up-to-date on what's happening with their kids) and a club record book, in which we keep track of our clients' names and addresses and other info, as well as our own schedules.

Sounds simple, doesn't it? It is. That's the beauty of it. And the amazing thing is that Kristy (the assertive friend I mentioned earlier) dreamed the whole thing up: meetings, Kid-Kits, notebook, and all. That's why she's president.

If we worked on a cruise ship, Kristy would have to be the cruise director. She's great at seeing the big picture and terrific at organizing people to carry out her ideas. Kristy's a born leader, and she's been that way all her life. I know, because we've been friends since we were in diapers. Which is surprising, in a way, because our personalities are so different. I'm as shy as she is bold, as quiet as she is rowdy. Maybe it's just a case of opposites attracting. We do look alike, at least. Kristy is also on the short side, with brown hair and brown eyes. She cares less about clothes than I do — less than anyone I know, actually. You rarely see her wearing anything but a T-shirt and shorts in the summer, a turtleneck and jeans in the winter.

Kristy's family life may be even more complicated than mine. She has two older brothers, Charlie and Sam, plus a younger one named David Michael. Back when David Michael was a baby, Kristy's dad walked out on the family. So Mrs. Thomas raised the kids on her own. (You can see where Kristy's grit and determination come from.) Then, after years of struggling along, Mrs. Thomas met and married a really nice guy, Watson Brewer, who happens to be a millionaire. So now the Thomas-Brewer clan lives in Watson's mansion, which is across town from where Kristy and I grew up. They share the mansion with Nannie, Kristy's grandmother, who moved in shortly after Kristy's mom and Watson adopted Emily Michelle, the world's cutest toddler (she was born in Vietnam). Nannie helps take care of Emily while everybody else is at work or school. Watson also has two kids from his first marriage, Karen and Andrew, who live there every other month.

They bring their pets along, adding them to the regular menagerie, which includes a grouchy, geriatric cat and a big, bouncy puppy.

Basically, it's a mob scene. And Kristy thrives on the chaos. (I'd probably spend a lot of time hiding in my room, hoping for peace and quiet.) She even looks for more stuff to keep her busy, such as special BSC projects, or the Krushers, which is a little kids' softball team she coaches.

Who would Kristy the Cruise Director pick for her assistant? Me, probably. Partly because we're best friends, and partly because I'm very good at keeping track of details. I'm the BSC's secretary, and I pride myself on keeping the record book one hundred percent up-to-date at all times. I know every member's schedule. I know every client's address, or at least I know where to look it up. And I have a handle on every one of our charges' allergies, food preferences, and favorite games. I'd have no trouble keeping tabs on a shipful of people.

The creative director for our cruise ship would have to be Claudia Kishi, the club's vice-president. Suppose some passengers wanted to put on a play. Claudia could paint the sets, make the costumes, and design a program in no time flat. As vice-president of the BSC, Claudia's creative urges are mostly funneled into supplying the best, most varied menu of munchies any club has ever seen. We meet in Claudia's room, since she has her own phone with a private line, and she always has plenty of junk food on hand. That is, if she can find it. Since her parents aren't crazy about her eating habits, the stuff is usually hidden away, along with the Nancy Drew mysteries of which her parents also disapprove.

Claudia is Japanese-American, with beautiful, long black hair and almond-shaped, dark eyes. And while she does happen to be a creative genius she's far from an academic genius like her older sister, Janine. In fact, Claudia's had so much trouble in school that she has to repeat seventh grade. She's not dumb; it's just that she doesn't care much about things like science or algebra.

Her best friend, Stacey McGill, on the other hand, is a math whiz, which is why she's the club's treasurer. (She'd make a great purser for our ship.) Keeping track of our funds and collecting dues each week is a breeze for her. (We use the dues to pay for such things as Claudia's phone bill.) Stacey has blonde, curly hair, blue eyes, and an incredible sense of style.

Stacey grew up in Manhattan, which is Fashion City. Her parents are divorced, and Stacey (an only child) lives here with her mom, though she visits her dad often. He still lives in the city, so her visits give her the chance to drop into Bloomingdale's on a regular basis. Her wardrobe reflects the fact that she's practically a professional shopper. Stacey is the trendiest, most sophisticated dresser in our school.

Stacey's not shallow, though. There's more to her than meets the eye. She has an inner strength I really admire. See, Stacey has diabetes, which is a lifelong disease. Her body doesn't process sugars correctly, which means not only that Stacey has to be very careful about what she eats and when she eats it, but that she has to give herself injections of insulin every day. If she doesn't take good care of herself, she can become very sick very quickly. But Stacey handles her diabetes with maturity. The rest of us in the BSC try to support her — for example, Claudia always has sugarless snacks on hand for her — but in the end only Stacey can take care of herself. And she does a great job of it.

Abby Stevenson takes care of herself, too. Like Stacey, she has a lifelong health problem. In her case, it's asthma plus allergies. But Abby doesn't let her asthma slow her down. She's a whirlwind of activity, always laughing and joking and running circles around everyone else.

Abby moved to Stoneybrook recently, along with her twin sister, Anna, and their mom. Anna and Abby are identical twins, so naturally they look a lot alike, with their thick, dark, curly hair and glasses (sometimes they wear contacts). But nobody has trouble telling them apart. They wear their hair differently, for one thing. Anna's is short and Abby's is long. And their personalities are different. Anna is more serious, especially about her music. She's a talented violinist and practices all the time. We asked both twins to join the BSC when they moved here, but only Abby felt she had the time.

Anna and Abby's dad died when they were nine. Abby doesn't talk about him much. I have a feeling it would make her too sad. And Abby doesn't spend much time being sad. She's full of fun and games. In fact, I think she'd make a perfect athletic director for our cruise ship. Abby loves sports and is a natural athlete — or at least, that's what Kristy, who would know, tells me.

Abby is our club's alternate officer, a job that used to belong to Dawn before she moved away. If any officer can't make it to a meeting, Abby takes over her duties.

The BSC also has two junior officers who are younger than the rest of us. Everyone I've mentioned so far is thirteen, but Mal and Jessi are eleven. They aren't allowed to baby-sit at night unless it's for their own families, but they take plenty of afternoon jobs.

Mallory Pike would be the perfect story-hour person for our ship's day care center. First of all, she's great with kids. She's the oldest of eight siblings. Vanessa, Nicky, Jordan, Byron, Adam, Margo, and Claire are the other seven. Try saying their names in under two seconds the way Mal can. So Mal has plenty of experience. Second, she's the best storyteller of all of us. She'd like to write and illustrate children's books someday. Mal is white, with reddish-brown hair and wears glasses and braces, both of which she hates.

Jessi Ramsey, Mal's best friend, is African-American, with black hair and dark, dark eyes. She'd make an excellent aerobics teacher for our ship's workout center. Jessi is in great physical shape because she studies ballet. She has a younger sister named Becca and a baby brother known as Squirt. Her parents both work, so her aunt Cecelia moved in with the family to help out.

Now you've met everyone in the BSC. Oops, that's not exactly true. I almost forgot about our associate members, who don't come to meetings but who are on call for those times when we're overwhelmed with work. One of them is Shannon Kilbourne, who lives in Kristy and Abby's neighborhood and goes to private school. The other is Logan. He's an excellent baby-sitter because he's so patient and kind.

Anyway, back to our meeting the day after Granny and Pop-Pop headed out to sea. Remember how I was wondering about what could possibly ruin their trip? Well, try this: a house full of water.

That's right. Something went very, very wrong with their plumbing and their house was flooded, not even twenty-four hours after they left! Sharon heard about it from a neighbor who was keeping an eye on the house. She called during our BSC meeting to ask a favor.

"I know it's not your usual type of job," Sharon told Kristy when she called. "I've already been in touch with my parents over a shipboard phone and told them I'd take some time off from work and handle everything. I don't want them to cut their trip short. But I'll need help. Would the BSC be willing to be part of my cleanup crew? I'll pay your usual fees."

Of course, we agreed. I pulled out the record book and drew up a schedule, making sure that at least one club member would be on hand every day for as long as the job took. I planned things so that I'd be there most of the time, especially for the next few days when everybody else was already booked up with jobs. We'd see to it that Granny and Pop-Pop's house was back to normal by the time they returned. From ship's crew to janitorial staff was quite a change, but my fantasy would have to be put on hold for awhile longer. The BSC had work to do.

CHAPTER 3

"Oh, Sharon," I said. I couldn't seem to say anything else. But Sharon understood.

"I know," she answered. "I know. It's awful, isn't it?"

It was Saturday morning, and we were sitting on the bottom step of Granny and Pop-Pop's basement stairs. It was the first time I'd been over there since the flood, and I couldn't believe my eyes. The damage was far, far worse than anything I'd imagined.

Granny and Pop-Pop use their basement quite a bit. It includes a rec room, the downstairs bathroom, and the spare bedroom that Pop-Pop uses as an office ever since he retired.

Sharon had called our plumber as soon as she'd learned of the flood. He and his crew had turned off the main valve, pumped out most of the water (it had been over a foot deep in some parts of the basement!), and vacuumed out some more, but that was all they'd had time to do. They'd be coming back on Monday to figure out what had gone wrong, assess the damage to the plumbing, and start work on fixing it. Until then, we were on our own.

"I don't even know where to start," said Sharon, shaking her head as she looked around. She sounded as if she were in shock.

Me? I was still speechless. I knew how Granny and Pop-Pop felt about their little house. "It's our nest," Granny would say lovingly, whenever someone complimented her on some curtains she'd made or on the way she'd decorated. And Pop-Pop was proud of the way he kept up the place, doing whatever small tasks were needed himself instead of hiring someone the way many of their friends did. He'd worked hard on converting the rec room into a cozy space for entertaining, and he'd built some of the shelves and cabinets in his office himself, hammering and sawing his evenings away in the tiny workshop he'd set up in a corner of the basement.

From our perch on the stairs I could tell that there was still plenty of moisture in the basement. The musty smell was the first clue. Also, the carpet was about three shades darker than its usual light blue, so I knew it was saturated. Clumps of sopping-wet magazines and newspapers were strewn around the floor. I saw a wicker wastebasket that I knew belonged in the bathroom. It must have floated out when the water was high.

I sighed. We had our work cut out for us.

Sharon stood up. "Well, let's take a look around and see if we can figure out what to do first," she said.

We stepped onto the carpet, and I felt it squish beneath my sneakers. "This carpet is going to have to come out," I said. "Do you think it can be dried and saved?"

Sharon shrugged. "I think that's a question we're going to be asking a lot today," she said. "And I have a feeling that in many cases the answer is going to be no. Water damage is hard to overcome."

We squished down the hall and into the rec room.

"Oh, boy," muttered Sharon.

"Ugh," I said. "What a mess."

The tan plaid couch was soaked at least halfway up, and so was the matching recliner. The legs of the coffee table showed where the high-water mark had been. The beautiful hooked rug Granny had worked on all last winter — a floral pattern featuring roses and ivy — was ruined beyond repair.

"The TV and the stereo look okay," said Sharon. "Good thing they're up high."

When she said "stereo," I had an awful thought. "What about the records?" I asked.

Granny and Pop-Pop have a huge collection of old records, mostly from when they were younger. They love to come down to the rec room after dinner, put on a stack of their big-band albums, and dance a few turns around the room. I've seen them do it more than once, and I've always thought it was so romantic.

"Doesn't look good," commented Sharon, pointing to the floor-level shelving beneath the stereo cabinet. All the records were stored there, which meant they'd all been underwater. "But maybe they can be salvaged," she went on. "We'll come back to them." I knew she wanted to keep going until we had a complete understanding of the damage.

We looked around some more.

"It's lucky those photo albums happened to be up there," I said, indicating a higher shelf. A large shelving unit filled one wall of the rec room, and everything on the upper shelves was dry.

"Oh, Granny would have been devastated to lose those," said Sharon with relief. "Let's take them upstairs today to make sure they don't absorb any more moisture than they already have. It's so damp down here."

I realized I was going to be doing a lot of carrying over the next few days. Practically everything that could be moved would have to be taken out of the basement so it would have a chance to dry. Fortunately, we'd been having a spell of sunny days. With luck, the weather would hold and we'd be able to dry things quickly by bringing them outside.

"These games are a total loss," said Sharon, pointing to a stack of board games piled on a lower shelf. Their cardboard boxes were soaked and peeling. "Somehow I don't think Granny will mind very much. I kind of doubt she and Pop-Pop have been playing Clue too often lately." She grinned at me, and I giggled. We would need to keep our sense of humor as we worked.

"Can you imagine Pop-Pop insisting to Granny that it was Colonel Mustard, in the library, with a candlestick?" I asked. I knew Granny and Pop-Pop had kept the games around for kids who visited, but it was funny to picture the two of them rolling dice and moving pieces around a board.

Once we'd checked out the rec room, we moved on to the bathroom. Since it's all tiled, there wasn't much damage, except for the wastebasket floating off. You could see the marks where the water had been, and everything would need a good cleaning, but nothing was ruined.

The spare bedroom was another story. It was a disaster. I nearly cried when I saw the beautiful quilt Granny had made, soaked from the bottom up. (The quilt was long enough to reach the floor.) The colors were running and the quilt lay limply on the bed. "What a shame," I said. But Sharon wasn't listening or paying any attention to the quilt.

Her gaze had gone to the tall, four-drawer file cabinet next to Pop-Pop's desk on the other side of the room. She practically ran to it and yanked open one of the bottom drawers. She pulled out a dripping-wet bundle of papers and tossed it aside. "Old tax records," she said over her shoulder. "Pop-Pop saved them longer than he needed to." She opened the next drawer and peered inside. "Files from his last job," she said. "They're pretty damp but they look okay. He can go through them and salvage anything important."

Then she pulled open the drawer above that one, looked inside, and let out a huge sigh of relief. "Dry," she said. "Thank goodness."

"What's in there?" I asked, curious.

"History," said Sharon quietly. "Granny and Pop-Pop's letters and papers. From the time they were kids and writing childish notes to friends and relations, all the way through until today. They probably fill up this top drawer, too." She pulled the drawer open, looked inside, and nodded.

"Wow," I said. "I never knew they were here."

26

"I did," said Sharon. "And I've always meant to help Granny and Pop-Pop sort and preserve them. I've been kicking myself ever since I heard about the flood. I was afraid they'd been lost forever."

"It's a good thing they weren't in the bottom drawers," I said.

"A very good thing," agreed Sharon. "And this time I'm going to make sure they're safe." She shut the drawers. "We'll take them upstairs today. That'll be a start, anyway." Then she turned to look around at the rest of the room. "So what else is ruined in here?" she asked.

We took a quick inventory. The bottom drawer of the dresser had been underwater, but it hadn't held anything more than mothballs. Another hooked rug, this one with a moon-and-stars design, had been soaked and possibly ruined. And Pop-Pop's entire collection of old *National Geographic* magazines, which had taken up the whole bottom shelf of a long bookcase, had turned into a soggy, pulpy mess.

"Well," said Sharon, "I guess it's time to start working." She gave me a smile. "I'm glad we wore old clothes. It's going to be a messy job."

"Where should we begin?" I asked.

Sharon considered for a moment. "I think we'll need help with heavy jobs like taking up the carpet and moving big pieces of furniture," she said. "For now, let's concentrate on taking the lighter items upstairs. We can begin with everything that's damp but not ruined. The stuff that's soaked can wait, and so can the dry things, except for those letters. I'll take them up on my first trip."

We decided to stow everything on the little screened-in sunporch, where it could stay if the weather turned bad. During sunny days, we could put things outside to dry.

"I'm starting in here," said Sharon. "Why don't you tackle the stuff on the shelves in the rec room?" She reached into a pocket of the apron she was wearing and pulled out two pairs of yellow rubber gloves. "These might be a good idea," she said, handing me a pair.

Those gloves were *definitely* a good idea. You wouldn't believe what a mess water can make! I found out as soon as I started pulling things off the shelves. Books would come apart in my hands. Magazines were like slimy sea creatures. That musty odor was even stronger now. And the shelves themselves were showing signs of water damage. The longer I worked, the more I realized what a huge job we had in front of us. It wasn't going to be easy to bring Granny and Pop-Pop's house back to its normal state.

After I'd worked awhile on the shelves, I turned to the records, carrying loads of them up the stairs. Fifteen loads, to be exact. Records are heavy, and *wet* records are even worse. And Granny and Pop-Pop own a lot of records.

When I finally finished with the records I went back to the shelves. I'd just finished clearing one of the lower ones when I noticed something odd about the paneled wall that provided the backing for the shelving unit. In one spot, the paneling looked a little crooked. Just a little. It was nothing you'd ever notice, as long as the shelf was full. I reached back to touch it, and a piece of the paneling fell forward, revealing a space behind it. A little cubbyhole. What could be inside? I reached in and felt around. At first I thought the space was empty. Then my hand found a corner of something, and I reached in deeper with both hands and pulled out a box.

A tightly wrapped, slightly soggy box about the size and shape of a toaster. I turned it over in my hands. Then I gasped. Written across the top in bold black letters (a little runny from the dampness) was the following warning:

DO NOT OPEN OR YOU WILL BE CURSED

CHAPTER 4

I didn't.

Open the wrapper, that is.

Not right away, anyway. I mean, sometimes I wonder if things like curses should be taken seriously. I fitted the piece of paneling back in place, put the wrapped box aside, and kept on working, clearing off shelves and carrying things upstairs. I must have passed Sharon on the stairs six or seven times, but I didn't say a word to her about what I'd found. Somehow I just wanted to keep it to myself and think about it for awhile.

And think about it is just what I did. Fortunately, the work I was doing didn't take much brain power. If it had, I would have been in trouble. All I could concentrate on was that mysterious package. What was inside it? Who had hidden it in the wall, and why? What if I were to open it? Would I really be cursed? What kind of curse would it be?

Opening it was probably worth the risk, since curses aren't usually real anyway. Right? I mean, how many people do you know who have actually been cursed?

Plus, if I didn't open the wrapper, whatever was inside would probably be ruined. It needed a chance to dry, just like everything else that had been in the basement. Curse or no curse, maybe it was my responsibility to open that wrapper.

All these thoughts were going through my head as I made my trips up and down the stairs, and finally I gave in. I picked up the box and set it on top of the stereo cabinet. Then, after taking a deep breath, I began to unwrap it.

Immediately, my hair turned white, my fingernails grew three inches, and every bone in my body began to ache.

Just kidding. Actually, nothing happened. Instead, the wrappings fell away to reveal a beautiful little chest covered with fancy carvings of flowers and vines.

I put the wrappings aside and took a closer look at the chest. I traced the carvings with my finger, marveling at how intricate they were. Every petal and leaf looked real. I'd never seen carving like that.

The box had a gold clasp on one side and hinges on the other. I didn't see any kind of lock. Obviously, I could open the chest if I wanted to. Did I want to? I wasn't sure. I couldn't help thinking about that curse. Maybe I'd gone far enough by opening the wrapper. Maybe I would just be asking for trouble if I opened the chest as well.

I picked up the wrapper again and examined the handwriting on it. It didn't look familiar. As far as I knew, the writing was neither Granny's nor Pop-Pop's. Nor was it Sharon's. And anyway, that curse stuff just wasn't her style. Who had this chest belonged to, and why had that person hidden it?

"Whew! I'm ready to quit for the day. How about you?"

I jumped at the sound of Sharon's voice. She had appeared in the doorway of the rec room. She wiped her brow and smiled at me. For a second, I was tempted to hide the little mahogany chest. It felt like a secret I wasn't sure I wanted to share. But instead, I heard myself asking her about it.

"See what I found?" I said, holding it up. "It was sort of hidden away." I didn't mention the wrapper or the warning.

"It's lovely," said Sharon, coming closer to take a better look. "All those carvings!"

"You've never seen it before?" I asked.

She shook her head. "Never. I don't think it belongs to either of my parents."

That was interesting. If Sharon didn't recognize it, the box must have been hidden for quite some time. "Is it okay if I take it home for a little while?" I asked. "It's so pretty. I want to make sure it's safe."

Sharon shrugged. "Sure," she said. "When Granny and Pop-Pop come home, we can ask them about it."

Sharon and I worked at the house all weekend, and I was so tired each night that I fell into bed. Still, I thought about the mahogany chest a lot. I wanted to open it, and yet I wasn't sure I should. I wanted to tell my friends about it, but somehow I also wanted to keep it a secret. The box sat on my dressing table, where I could see it from my bed. It was the first thing I saw in the morning and the last thing I saw at night.

Early on Monday morning, Sharon and I met Jim Prentice, the plumber, at Granny and Pop-Pop's house.

Sharon invited Jim to have a cup of coffee before he started work. We'd picked up some doughnuts on our way to the house. The three of us sat around the kitchen table, and Sharon told Jim about the work we'd done over the weekend.

He shook his head. "It's a shame," he said. "I have to admit I was a little upset when I saw how bad things looked here the other day. You see, I grew up across the street." He smiled shyly. "My family lived there from the time I was born until I was nine or ten years old. Which is a long time ago. I had a friend who lived in this house and I was over here a lot. Coming back to this block was like coming home."

"Well, isn't that a coincidence!" said Sharon. "You know, it's funny. I think this neighborhood has a hold on people. My mother actually grew up in the house next door to this one."

"Really?" I asked. "I never knew that."

Sharon nodded. "When she and Pop-Pop married and returned to Stoneybrook, Granny hoped to move back into that house, but it wasn't for sale. This one was, though, so they bought it."

I tried to imagine Granny and Pop-Pop as newlyweds, sitting in this same sunny kitchen.

Jim and Sharon talked about the neighborhood for awhile longer and then Jim pushed back his chair, thanked us for the doughnuts and coffee, and said he'd better go downstairs and try to figure out what had gone wrong.

While Jim poked around in the unfinished part of the basement, where the water heater and the furnace and all the pipes are, Sharon and I went back to our routine. We carried things up the stairs and spread them out on the lawn to dry if they seemed salvageable, or tossed them into the garbage (we'd already filled four cans) if not.

About an hour later, Jim appeared in the doorway of the rec room, where Sharon and I were working. He wiped his hands on a rag before he spoke. He looked very serious. "This is not going to be a small job," he told Sharon. "I hate to say it, but I think it's going to take awhile."

"What went wrong, exactly?" asked Sharon.

"It has to do with a valve that ruptured," Jim explained. "There's a valve that controls the pressure of the water coming in from the town system, and it broke. That's what caused the flooding. But there's a good bit of very old-fashioned plumbing in this house. If the house were being built today, it wouldn't pass the building codes. The whole system needs updating, or else there are going to be even bigger problems down the line." He twisted the rag in his hands. I could tell he hated giving Sharon the bad news.

Sharon sighed. "Well, if that's the situation, that's the situation," she said. "We might as well do what we can while my parents are away and save them the bother and mess."

"My thoughts exactly," said Jim. "Also, I notice you might need a contractor in here, too, to fix up some of these shelves and cabinets that were damaged." He waved a hand around, and Sharon nodded. "My crew works with a good contractor. In fact, we're finishing up a job together right now, an addition over on Chestnut Drive. Eddie has a week or two off before his next job, so I bet he'd be interested in this one. Anyway, we could start putting in a few hours a day over here right away, and then as soon as we finish our other job we'll be here full-time."

Sharon nodded. "That would be great," she said.

I cleared my throat. "That job on Chestnut Drive — is that the Barrett-DeWitt house?" I asked.

Jim smiled. "Sure is," he said. "Do you know those kids?"

"I baby-sit for them all the time." The BSC members sit for the Barrett-DeWitt family regularly, which is how I knew they were having an addition built onto their house.

"Bet they keep you busy," said Jim with a grin.

"They sure do," I answered. "All seven of them."

"Only seven? I was positive there were at least a dozen."

"I'm sure this job will seem quiet in comparison," said Sharon. Then she and Jim talked awhile more about what needed to be done, and he promised to bring Eddie by the next morning. It looked as if we were on our way to bringing the house back to normal.

That night at dinner, Sharon told my dad about what Jim had discovered. Then we talked about how the cleanup was going. Sharon was feeling upbeat. "I'm just glad we were able to salvage so much," she said. "And I'm especially happy that we found those letters." She'd already told my dad about discovering the letters in a dry file drawer. "I would have been so upset if they'd been ruined," she went on. "But now that they're safe and sound, I have a great idea. I think we should put them in a scrapbook as an anniversary present. Want to help, Mary Anne?"

I nodded. "I'd love to," I said.

Later, in my room, I thought about how interesting it would be to go through Granny and Pop-Pop's correspondence. I remembered the last time I'd looked through old letters. I'd discovered the truth about what had happened after my mother died. That had been quite a shock, but nothing like that was going to surface when I looked over Granny and Pop-Pop's letters. After all, they weren't even related to me by blood. I would just have a glimpse into history, and that sounded like fun.

Thinking of history reminded me of the mahogany chest. I glanced at it, sitting there on my dressing table. I still hadn't told my friends about it. I'd kept my mouth shut during our BSC meeting that day, even when the subject of Granny and Pop-Pop's house came up. Now, all of a sudden, I just couldn't control my curiosity anymore. Curse or no curse, I had to open it. And when I did, I had the surprise of my life.

The little mahogany chest was a music box. And it still worked.

The second its lid was opened, the music began to play. The song was "Twinkle, Twinkle, Little Star," and every note was clear and bright.

CHAPTER 5

monday

I think we should invite Eddie to be an honorary member of the BSC, don't you?

He definitely qualifies. He's patient, understanding, great with kids... but I think he already has his hands full as far as work goes.

True. Anyway, I'm not sure what some of our regular clients would think if their new sitter showed up wearing work boots, a tool belt, and a beard!

While I was working at Granny and Pop-Pop's that Monday afternoon, Jessi and Abby were sitting (actually it was more like doing crowd control, Abby told me later) over at the Barrett-DeWitts'.

"Oh, thank goodness you're here," said Mrs. DeWitt when she opened the door for Jessi and Abby that morning. As always, Mrs. DeWitt looked gorgeous. She was wearing a casual silk shirt and jeans, and her long auburn hair hung in shining waves down her back. (Mrs. DeWitt looked like a model, no kidding.) "Come on in, quick. I left the water running in the kitchen sink."

Jessi and Abby glanced at each other as they followed her into the house. It's not always a great sign when a parent is *that* happy to see a sitter.

"Things are just crazy around here," Mrs. DeWitt called over her shoulder as she led them into the kitchen.

Jessi and Abby glanced at each other again. Jessi told me later that something in Mrs. De-Witt's voice reminded her of when we BSC members first started sitting for the Barretts. Mrs. DeWitt was newly divorced — we knew her as Mrs. Barrett back then — and her life was always topsy-turvy. Her house was a mess, she was totally disorganized, and the kids were running wild. So wild, in fact, that we used to call them "The Impossible Three." The Barrett kids are Buddy, who's eight, Suzi, who's five, and Marnie, who's only two. They're great kids, but even great kids can react badly when their lives are turned upside down.

Since that time their mom has pulled herself together, and the kids have calmed down. Also, she is now remarried, to Franklin DeWitt, a father of four: Lindsey, who's eight; Taylor, who's six; four-year-old Madeleine; and Ryan, who's the same age as Marnie. Over time, the seven kids have learned to like each other, and the family runs surprisingly smooth.

Not long ago, the Barrett-DeWitts moved into a new house (new to them, that is) over by Stoneybrook Elementary School. The kids had insisted on staying in Stoneybrook, even though it was hard for their parents to find a house that was both big enough and affordable. The house they ended up falling in love with and buying had only four bedrooms, which is why they were having an addition constructed.

Jessi and Abby had seen the trucks in the driveway when they arrived. Now they heard the hammering and sawing and found plaster dust covering everything. One look out the kitchen window told them that the backyard was a muddy mess filled with wood scraps and discarded pieces of wallboard. They were in a construction zone, all right.

"Abby! Jessi!" Suzi appeared in the doorway, looking excited. "Guess what? Lindsey and me and Madeleine are going to have our very own bedroom."

"I," corrected her mother, distractedly.

"I and Lindsey and Madeleine are going to have our own room!" Suzi said obediently.

Her mom just smiled and shook her head.

Suzi went on. "Isn't that cool. And we can decorate it any way we want. And Eddie is putting a secret door in the wall, but don't tell, because it's a secret."

Too excited to stand still, she dashed off without waiting for a response.

"Who's Eddie?" asked Jessi.

"Our contractor," said Mrs. DeWitt. "He's terrific. He's been able to figure out how to do everything we wanted. And he's great with the kids." Suddenly, she put her hand to her mouth. "That reminds me. The reason I was so glad to see you is that we seem to be having a kid convention here today. I forgot it was my day to have the Kuhn kids over — Mrs. Kuhn and I have sort of a trade-off arrangement — and I told my kids they could invite a couple of friends to our house. They're so excited about the construction, and they love to show their friends what's going on here. So anyway, three of the Pike kids are coming, too." Mrs. DeWitt looked a little sheepish. "Naturally, I'll pay you whatever you think is fair for the time you spend here today."

Jessi was busy counting in her head. Seven Barrett and DeWitt kids, plus the three Kuhn children, plus three Pikes — "Yikes!" she said aloud. "Thirteen kids. We could probably use a couple more sitters. May I use your phone? Maybe Mal and Claudia could come over."

Abby just grinned. She loves a challenge. She started brainstorming, trying to think up some good group activities. By the time Jessi finished her phone call and gave the thumbs-up sign, meaning that Claud and Mal would be accompanying the Pike kids, Abby had already planned a day's worth of fun.

There was only one thing she hadn't counted on.

The kids had their own ideas.

The Kuhns were the first to arrive. As Jessi and Abby welcomed the kids, they overheard parts of a conversation between Mrs. Kuhn and Mrs. DeWitt.

" . . . doesn't seem like such a good time, with the construction and all . . ." Mrs. Kuhn was saying.

But Mrs. DeWitt was telling her it was fine for the kids to visit. " . . . all excited about showing off their new rooms . . ." Abby heard her say.

Meanwhile, the Barrett and DeWitt kids swarmed downstairs to greet their friends. Jake, who's eight, had brought his softball glove with him, and he held it up to show Buddy. Six-year-old Laurel smiled shyly at Lindsey. And Patsy, who's five, gave Suzi a huge grin. The Barrett and Kuhn kids have been friends for awhile. Buddy and Suzi and the three Kuhns are all members of Kristy's Krushers, the softball team Kristy manages. But the DeWitt kids have had no trouble making friends. In fact, when they first met, Laurel immediately gravitated toward Lindsey. Laurel likes to think she's super-mature — especially compared to Patsy — and having a playmate who's two years older suits her just fine.

Soon after the Kuhns settled in, Mrs. DeWitt left for work. (She has a part-time job.) And not long after that, Mrs. Pike dropped off her gang. Jessi and Abby were relieved to see Mal and Claudia with them, especially since the Pike kids seemed to be in a squabbling mood.

"I don't *care* if you barf in the car," Nicky (who's eight) was saying to Margo as they entered. "It's not fair that you always get to sit in front."

"No fair!" echoed Claire, who's five and hates it when things aren't fair. "No fair, no fair, nofe air!" she began to chant, until Mal put a hand on her shoulder.

"But I can't help it," wailed Margo, who's seven and has a notoriously weak stomach. "It's not my fault!"

"And Dad *does* care if she barfs in the car," Mal reminded Nicky. "So you'll just have to learn to like riding in the backseat." She turned to Abby and Jessi and rolled her eyes. "May I present my adorable siblings?" she asked, grinning.

"Charmed, I'm sure," replied Abby, giving a little bow.

"Delighted," said Jessi. She performed an elegant ballerina's curtsy.

The three younger Pikes ignored them.

"So, is your room almost done?" Nicky asked Buddy.

"Almost. Eddie's putting in the windows today. Want to see?"

"I do! I do!" yelled Claire.

"How about if we all take the tour together," Abby suggested, thinking it would be best for the kids to troop through the construction site all at once instead of in twos and threes. She'd already given up the plans she'd made for the day. Obviously the kids were only interested in the new addition.

"Yea!" everybody shouted. Buddy led the charge up the stairs. The sitters looked at one another, shrugged, and laughed. Then they trooped along behind the kids.

Jessi expected the contractors to be irritated by the interruption, but she couldn't have been more wrong. By the time she, Mal, Claud, and Abby arrived in the first of the unfinished rooms, they found a bearded man, who they knew must be Eddie, entertaining the crowd by showing how fast he could bang a nail into a two-by-four.

"Do another one!" Margo insisted when the first nail had disappeared.

"No, show them how you sharpen a pencil with your knife," suggested Buddy. "Eddie knows how to do everything," he said to Nicky. "He can build anything in the whole world."

Eddie smiled up at the kids. "My brother might disagree with that," he said. "Right, Jake?" he called.

"Ask him about the airplane he built when we were little," answered a voice from the room next door.

Eddie laughed. "It looked good, but it wasn't so great at flying. "I'd like to try that again sometime."

"Just don't ask me to be a passenger," teased a blonde woman in jeans, a T-shirt, and work boots. She was working in a corner, fitting some wallboard around a closet doorway.

"Aw, Lori, don't you trust your old boss?"

asked Eddie, pretending to be hurt. The kids were charmed.

"Eddie, can we help you today?" asked Buddy.

"Can we?" pleaded Suzi. "I could hold a hammer!" She gave Eddie her best dimpled smile.

"I don't know, kids, we're pretty busy in here today," said Eddie. "Trying to finish up so you'll have your rooms all ready, you know?" He stroked his beard. "Tell you what. How about if I set you up with a project of your own?"

"Yea!" shouted the kids.

"Let's make an airplane!" suggested Nicky.

"I was thinking more of . . ." Eddie paused tantalizingly, ". . . a playhouse. Something you could have out in the backyard. You could work on it in that old shed, and once it's done you'll have it forever."

"Really? You would help us?" asked Buddy.

"Sure, pal."

Jessi knew that he was offering this idea partly as a way to keep the kids out of his hair. She also knew he didn't have to do it. Her admiration for him grew as she watched him sketch a plan for the building and instruct the older kids on how to safely scavenge scrap lumber from the pile in the back of the house.

The rest of the afternoon flew by as the kids

became engrossed in their work. Jessi, Abby, Claud, and Mal made sure to thank Eddie as they left. They'd never seen anyone handle thirteen kids so easily, and they couldn't wait to tell Kristy and the rest of us about the super sitter they'd met.

CHAPTER 6

The sailor was so sad. That was what I couldn't forget. His sad, sad eyes. They were a deep blue, almost matching the trim on his sparkling white uniform.

Who was he? I wish I knew.

I woke up on Tuesday morning feeling unsettled. I'd been dreaming — all night, or at least it seemed that way — about this sad young sailor boy, dressed in a World War II uniform. He appeared everywhere in my dreams that night. First I spotted him walking down a long hallway, between periods at school. Then he turned up at Pizza Express, while I was splitting a pizza with Logan and some of our friends. He popped out from behind a tree as I walked up to my house. He turned up in the soda aisle at the supermarket, in the auditorium during an assembly, and even in Claudia's room in the middle of a BSC meeting.

It was as if he wanted to be part of my everyday life. There I'd be in my dream, enjoying myself with my friends or just going through the motions of a regular afternoon — and he'd turn up. He'd always appear in the background, dressed in his sailor uniform and looking out of place. Apparently, only I could see him, since nobody else ever seemed to notice the silent, straight-backed figure in white.

Twice — no, three times — I tried to speak to him, to ask him who he was and what he wanted. Because it was clear that he wanted something. His sad eyes held a question that only I could answer. But what was that question?

I don't know. He looked as if he wanted to speak, as if he wanted to speak very badly. But when he opened his mouth, no words came out. And when I tried to ask him questions, my voice was also silenced. It was as if the two of us stood on opposite sides of some invisible wall.

And he was so very, very sad.

My heart went out to him, and more than anything I wanted to comfort him, to give the right answer to the question in his eyes. But I couldn't reach him. I couldn't hug him. And I couldn't make it all better.

I hate that! To me, there's nothing worse than seeing someone you care about (and somehow,

I did immediately care about this sailor boy) feeling bad. Usually I can make people feel better with a hug or some kind words. But this time I was powerless.

You probably think I'm nuts, right? Going on like this about a dream? The thing is, it's hard for me to explain how *real* the dream was. The sailor looked as familiar to me as an old friend, even though I couldn't figure out where I knew him from. And his presence in my dream was so vivid that I could see every button on his uniform, every detail of his face.

As I lay in bed that morning thinking about the dream, I heard the phone ring. That brought me back into the real world, and I sat up and stretched. Immediately, my eyes fell upon the music box sitting on my dresser, and I forgot about the mysterious sailor. Here was a *real* mystery. A beautiful music box, hidden away long ago. Who had hidden it, and why? I wanted to find out.

"Mary Anne!" called Sharon from downstairs. "Granny's on the phone. Would you like to say hello?"

I popped out of bed and pulled on my robe. "I'm coming!" I called. I ran out into the hall and picked up the upstairs phone. "Granny?" I said eagerly. "How are you? How's Pop-Pop? Are you having a good time?"

"We sure are," said Granny. "We're being

pampered like kings and queens. I don't know how I'll ever go back to doing my own cooking and cleaning. And we go dancing every single night. It's wonderful."

She sounded happy and relaxed. "Granny, I have to ask you something." I said suddenly, without stopping to think about it. "When I was working over at your house the other day I found a music box hidden away." I paused, wondering if she'd react.

Granny didn't say anything, so I went on. "It's really beautiful, and it plays 'Twinkle, Twinkle, Little Star.' I'm dying to know who it belonged to. Was it yours?"

"Mine?" asked Granny. Her voice sounded just a little bit strange, or was it the connection? Those ship-to-shore phones don't always have the clearest sound. "No — no, dear," she went on. "I don't know anything about a music box. No, it must have belonged to someone else. Someone who lived in the house before we did, perhaps." Granny's voice was fading out. "Anyway, it sounds like we're losing our connection. It's great to hear you!"

"It's great to hear you, too," I said.

We said our good-byes, and I hung up. I headed back into my room and looked at the music box again. The more I thought about it, the more curious I became. I just had to know its story. I decided to do some detective work. I knew I could count on my fellow BSC members for help. They love a mystery, and together we've solved more than one. I resolved to show them the music box and tell them about the mystery at our next BSC meeting.

Meanwhile, it was time to dress and head over to Granny and Pop-Pop's for another day of work. Claudia was going to help out, and I knew Sharon had a big day planned. The plumbers and contractors would be on hand for part of the day, which would mean even more upheaval as they tore out pipes and cabinets that would need replacing.

After a quick breakfast, Sharon and I drove over to the house, where we found work in full swing. The basement was bursting with noise and activity. Jim Prentice greeted us as we came down the stairs and introduced us to his assistant, Dooley, a small man with a crooked smile and a shock of white hair.

"Nice to meet you, Mr. Dooley," said Sharon.

"Pleasure to meet you, too — but it's just Dooley," said the man. "No mister necessary."

I never did find out if Dooley was his first name or his last.

What I did find out was that Dooley was a perfectionist. More than once that morning I saw him fiddling at great length over some tiny detail, frowning as he worked. Jim would try to hurry him along, but Dooley wouldn't be hurried. Not only was he a fussbudget, but he was convinced that his way was the only way.

"Can't rush a job like this," he'd say. "No point in doing it unless it's done just so." And he'd continue in his slow, methodical way.

Meanwhile, Eddie and his crew were like a tornado, ripping through the rooms in no time. I'd heard about Eddie at Monday's BSC meeting, so I wasn't surprised to find that he was friendly and outgoing.

"Hope you don't mind that we started right in," he told Sharon. "Jake, here, couldn't stand to wait another minute to pull out those cabinets, could you, Jake?"

Jake, who was straining hard as he worked to remove one of the water-damaged cabinets in the spare bedroom, grimaced.

"Jake can't stand taking orders from his big brother," Eddie confided to us in a stage whisper. "He's only working for me until he has enough money to start his own business. Isn't that right, Jake?"

"You bet, brother," grunted Jake, who had just worked the cabinet free. "And hopefully you'll come crawling to me asking for a job one day. I'd love to order you around for awhile!"

Eddie also introduced us to Lori, whom Abby, Jessi, Claud, and Mal had met at the Barrett-DeWitt job. Lori put down the pile of damaged shelving she was carrying in order to shake our hands. She wasn't big, but she was obviously very strong. She offered to help us move the couch and the other heavy furniture upstairs, and Sharon accepted immediately.

We started as soon as Claudia arrived. Lori showed us how to lift correctly, using our legs instead of our backs. Then she told us how we were going to move the couch up the stairs slowly, one step at a time. She put me and Claudia at the front, and she and Sharon took the back. "One, two, three," she counted, and we lifted.

The couch was heavy, but moving it wasn't impossible, not with the four of us working together. I felt a rush of pride as we reached the top of the stairs and put the couch down for a rest. "We did it!" I said.

"And you likely ruined your backs, too," I heard someone say behind me. I turned to see Hank and Esther. Good old Hank, always the optimist.

"Good morning, Hank, Esther," said Sharon, wiping her forehead with a bandanna she pulled out of her back pocket. "Nice to see you. What brings you over?"

"We just wanted to tell you how sorry we were to hear about the flooding," said Esther, "and we thought we'd drop off this coffee cake for you and the work crews." She held out a foil-wrapped package.

"Well, thanks! I know that will be appreciated," said Sharon.

"How bad is the damage?" asked Hank. "Will the insurance cover anything?"

"You can look around and see for yourself," said Sharon. "And yes, fortunately, my parents have excellent insurance."

Hank almost looked disappointed.

He and Esther headed downstairs while we finished moving the couch onto the screened porch. "If we're lucky, it'll dry out," said Sharon. "If not, well, it's an old couch."

Just then, Jim and Dooley came up the stairs, followed by Hank and Esther. "Heard a rumor about coffee cake," said Jim.

"It's true," said Sharon. "I was just about to invite everyone to share it." She began cutting up the cake. Jim cleared his throat.

"I'm afraid I have some not-so-good news," he said. "Some of the pipes going out to the main are beyond saving. We're going to have to replace them, which means we'll have to do some digging in the front and side yards, and probably even some of the back."

Something odd happened when he said that. I was standing next to Hank, and I felt him give a start. I glanced at him and saw him give Esther a significant look. What was *that* all about? Maybe he was just congratulating himself on the fact that all his most pessimistic predictions were coming true. I looked at Claud to see if she'd noticed, but she was too busy eyeing the coffee cake.

The rest of that morning was uneventful, except for one strange moment when I came into the now nearly empty spare bedroom, looking for a mop and bucket I'd misplaced. Someone was bent over the file cabinet, which, now that it was emptied, we'd left in the room. When he straightened up, I saw that it was Jim, and that he had a little notebook in his hand. What was he doing? There were no pipes in the bedroom and no plumbing. Why was he snooping around in the file cabinet? It was empty, but he didn't know that yet. Of course, I didn't ask any of those questions out loud. I was too shy.

When he saw me, he mumbled something and fled the room. I liked Jim Prentice, and I thought he was doing a great job. But from that moment on, I never quite felt I could trust him.

CHAPTER 7

"I just don't trust him," said Kristy, frowning. She was leaning back in Claudia's director's chair, chewing thoughtfully on the pencil she'd pulled from over her ear. "I'm telling you, something weird is going on over there."

It was Wednesday afternoon, and my friends and I were gathered in Claudia's room for a BSC meeting. Kristy was breaking her own rule about sticking to club business during meeting times, which meant that we were all free to talk about the mystery at Granny and Pop-Pop's.

Mystery? That's right. Kristy and I had spent the day working at the house and by the time we had left we were just about positive that we had a mystery on our hands. Kristy hit the nail on the head. Something weird was definitely going on at 747 Bertrand Drive. (That's Granny and Pop-Pop's address, in case you're wondering.)

I had another mystery on my mind, as well:

the mystery of the music box. I was waiting for the right moment to tell my friends about that one. And this wasn't it. For now, everybody was too interested in what Kristy was telling them.

"And it's not just Jim, either. Wait'll you hear what Mary Anne has to tell you about Eddie. And Jake," she went on.

"Don't forget Hank and Esther," I put in.

"I was just about to mention them," said Kristy. "Hank and Esther — and that old man. Who was he, and what was he doing there?"

I knew exactly what Kristy was talking about, but none of the others had a clue.

"Old man?" asked Claudia, who was sitting on her bed with her back against the wall and her feet on Stacey's lap. She was busy munching on a handful of Doritos. "What old man? I didn't see any old man when I was there."

"And who in the world are Hank and Esther?" asked Stacey, who sat between me and Claudia on the bed, dipping a brush into a tiny pink bottle. She was painting Claudia's toenails. She frowned as she concentrated on the little toe of Claudia's right foot. "I haven't heard of them. Are they part of Jim's crew?"

I had to laugh, imagining Hank and Esther under the kitchen sink, working on the plumbing. Hank would be grousing about something, and Esther would be her cheerful self as she banged away with a huge monkey wrench.

"What did Eddie do?" asked Abby. She crossed her arms and frowned, as if she were Eddie's only defender. "Eddie's the greatest. He couldn't have done anything wrong. I just *know* he couldn't have."

"You have to cross Jake off your suspect list, too," added Jessi, who was sitting cross-legged on the floor. "I've met him, and he's just a regular nice guy. I'm sure he's not involved."

"Involved in *what*?" asked Mal from her spot next to Jessi. "Everybody has to slow down here. I'm totally confused. Can we back up for a second? What are all these people being accused of, anyway?"

Kristy looked blank for a second. "Accused?" she asked. "Nobody accused them of anything. We just wonder what they're up to, that's all."

"And remind me, why is it that we think they're up to something?" asked Abby.

"Because of the way they're all snooping around," I burst out. "That's what this is all about." I couldn't blame my friends for being confused. Kristy and I hadn't explained things very well. "See, the first thing that happened was that I ran into Jim in the spare bedroom." I paused, letting that sink in.

"So?" asked Claudia.

"So why was he in there?" I asked. "There

aren't any pipes or anything in that room. And I think he was snooping in the file cabinet."

"That's odd," said Abby.

"See? That's what we're saying," said Kristy. "It's odd, that's all. And it was also odd when I caught Eddie out in the toolshed. I mean, there probably haven't been any tools in that shed for about a gazillion years. It's an old, broken-down thing. But I saw him go in there, so I followed him. He *said* he was looking for a shovel." Kristy raised her eyebrows. "Now, wouldn't you think that a guy with his own construction crew and his own big truck would bring his own shovel?"

"Maybe he forgot it," said Abby stoutly. She didn't want to hear a word against Eddie. "Or maybe his was the wrong size or something."

Kristy raised her eyebrows again. "I'm just saying that he was acting like a man with a secret," she said. "He jumped when I first came into the shed, and he had this guilty, furtive look about him."

"Furtive?" Abby repeated. "Come on."

Just then the phone rang. It was Mrs. DeWitt, confirming a date she'd made for Friday afternoon. She needed two sitters as usual. Stacey and Claudia agreed to go.

Kristy handled the call. As soon as she hung up, she returned to the subject of the mystery. "All right, forget about Eddie for a minute.

What about Jim? Wait until you hear what he said to Dooley."

There was more confusion until Kristy and I explained who Dooley was. Claudia chipped in her two cents. She'd met Dooley, too.

"I was just coming into the kitchen when I heard them talking," Kristy said. "Jim was holding that little notebook again, and this is what I heard him say." She paused for a big effect. "He said, 'I know it's around here somewhere. It has to be, unless the old man was lying.' " Kristy crossed her arms and, looking satisfied, sat back in her chair.

"And this proves — what?" asked Claudia with a grin.

"I'm not saying it proves anything," said Kristy. "It's just part of the puzzle."

"Along with the weird way Hank was acting," I said. "Hank is an old friend of my grandmother's," I explained hurriedly before anyone could ask. "And Esther is his wife. But it's Hank who's acting suspicious. He came over again today, and he seems very, very interested in the backyard. He keeps asking Jim all kinds of questions about exactly where he's going to be digging when he replaces those pipes. And today I caught him just gazing out the window, looking into the backyard with this very thoughtful expression on his face."

"Okay," said Mal, who had grabbed a notebook and was scribbling away, taking notes. She held up a hand and read back what she'd written. " 'Jim in bedroom. Eddie in toolshed. Jim says something about how "it" has to be around there somewhere. And Hank can't stay out of the backyard.' Is that it?"

"Not quite," I said. "But I'm glad you started putting this down in the mystery notebook. It definitely qualifies." The mystery notebook is another of Kristy's great ideas. The BSC members have always loved helping to solve mysteries, but for a long time we had no organized way of keeping track of suspects, clues, and theories. We'd write things down on napkins, math tests, whatever was at hand. Our record keeping was terrible. Then Kristy came up with the idea for one central notebook where we could write down everything. Ta-da! The mystery notebook was born.

"There is one more thing. The old man."

"Oh, right," said Kristy. "I almost forgot about him."

"Explain, please?" asked Stacey.

"There was this elderly man hanging around all day today," Kristy said. "I kept seeing him lurking near the backyard. He seemed very, very interested in the construction work going on. I even saw him pacing off the distance between the fence and that old apple tree. I can't figure out what he's after."

"Maybe he's just one of those bored retirees," suggested Abby. "You know, the ones who don't know what to do with themselves once they stop working. My grandfather was like that at first. My grandmother used to kick him out of the house because he'd just wander around complaining about how bored he was. So he'd take these long walks in the neighbor-hood — "

"Right," interrupted Kristy. I thought she was being a little rude, but Abby didn't seem to mind. "But I think there's more to the story with this guy. I tried to approach him a couple of times to say hi and find out if there was something he wanted to ask, but every time I would move toward him, he'd disappear in a flash."

"Hmmm," said Mal. "That does sound kind of suspicious."

Suspicious was the word of the day. Was it only a coincidence that so many people were acting so suspiciously? What *was* going on at 747 Bertrand Drive?

We talked about it for awhile, but none of us had any brilliant insights. Instead, we all agreed to keep an eye on the doings at Granny and Pop-Pop's house and to continue to write down any possible clues or suspects in the mystery notebook. Even though we hadn't come any closer to solving the mystery, our discussion had accomplished one good thing: Everybody was up-to-date on what was happening.

Just before our meeting ended, as our talk about the mystery wound down, I decided it was time to bring up the other mystery in my life: the mystery of the music box. Quietly, while the others were busy talking, I slipped it out of my backpack.

Claudia was the first to notice it. "Wow, look at that! Is it yours, Mary Anne?"

I shook my head. "Just temporarily," I said.

"It's really beautiful," said Stacey. "Whose is it?"

"I don't know. I wish I did." Then I explained everything. I told my friends where I'd found the box and when. I told them about what the wrapper around it had said, and how it had taken me awhile to work up the courage to open the box. Kristy seemed a little ticked off that I hadn't told her about the box right away, but she forgot about that when she heard it play.

When I lifted the cover and the first notes sounded, my friends fell silent. The song was so bright and innocent. It seemed to weave a spell around us.

I lifted the lid and played the song over and

over, and still nobody said a word. We were focused on the beautiful box and its tinkling tune.

Then, suddenly, I noticed something very odd. When I opened the box and looked inside, I could see that the inner compartment was much smaller than the outside of the box.

The inside was lined in dark green velvet. I took a closer look and noticed a tiny black tab, almost hidden by the deep nap of the fabric. I pinched it between my thumb and forefinger and pulled. To my surprise, the entire compartment lifted away to show another space, lined in dark green satin, beneath the first one.

And this second, very secret compartment was not empty.

CHAPTER 8

"Oh, my lord," I gasped, staring into the box.

"What is it?" asked Kristy.

"Is there something inside?" Claudia leaned over my shoulder. "Oh, cool. An old picture."

I was speechless, but I was sure my heart was pounding loudly enough to be heard on the next block. What was just an old picture to Claud was something much, much more to me.

The cracked and faded black-and-white photograph that lay face up on the smooth green satin was of a young man who looked about eighteen. Someone was in the picture next to him, but had been cut out, except for a hand and a wrist. On the wrist was an ID bracelet. I was pretty sure the person who had been cut out was a woman.

But it wasn't the bracelet or the woman's hand that made me feel as if I couldn't breathe. No, it was something else. It was the young man.

You may have trouble believing this.

I know I do.

But it's absolutely true.

The man in the picture was the same young man I'd been dreaming about. My sailor boy.

He wasn't wearing his white sailor suit, but there was no mistaking him for anybody else. I knew that face. His eyes weren't nearly as sad in this picture — was it because of the girl beside him? — but it was definitely him. Somehow the boy I'd been dreaming about was connected with the music box I'd found. How could that be? Was I going to be haunted by this sailor boy because I'd dared to ignore the warning and open the box?

"Mary Anne, are you okay?" Kristy asked. "You're white as a sheet. What's the matter?"

Her voice seemed to be coming from a long way off.

"Mary Anne?" she repeated. "Yo, Earth to Mary Anne!"

I shook my head, trying to clear it. "What? I mean, nothing's wrong. I'm fine." In a split second, I'd decided not to tell my friends why the person in that picture looked familiar to me. Why? Two reasons. One, they'd think I was out of my mind. Two, I needed some time to think about what it meant.

Kristy was still giving me a curious look. So were the rest of my friends. But I ignored them.

"Look, there's a letter, too," I said, trying to distract them. I held up the small envelope that was nestled beneath the picture. It was slightly yellowed with age, and there was no name or address on the front.

"Ooh! Open it," urged Mal. "What does it say?"

I hesitated. Was it ever really right to open and read someone else's mail without permission? "I don't know," I said.

"Mary *Anne*," said Kristy impatiently. "If you won't open it, hand it over."

"But — " I began.

Stacey took the letter out of my hand, and I let her. To be honest, I was just as curious as my friends were. Still, I felt better letting someone else do the actual opening.

The envelope wasn't sealed. Stacey lifted the flap and pulled out a sheet of unlined paper. "It's not really a letter," said Stacey. "It's more like a note." She read it quickly to herself. Then she sighed. "Wow, that's so romantic."

"What?" asked Claudia. "Let me see!"

"Read it out loud," said Abby. "We all want to hear."

"I think it went with the music box," said Stacey. "Somebody — the guy in the picture maybe? — gave the music box to somebody else, and this note was probably inside." She sighed again.

"Stacey," Kristy said with a warning tone in her voice.

I think Stacey was enjoying the drama of the situation, and I couldn't blame her. But she was driving the rest of us wild.

"Okay, okay." Stacey cleared her throat and read out loud. "It says, 'Dearest L. S., They're playing our song. Think of me whenever you look up at the night sky. I'll be on the other side of the world, thinking of you. And, before long, I'll be back and we can look at the stars together, forever.' " Stacey paused. "It's signed H. I. W."

We were silent for a second. Then I gave a huge sniff. I couldn't help it. The note was so romantic. And I couldn't help thinking that it must be from my sailor boy to a girl he loved. Did he ever come back? (I assumed he'd given her the music box before he left to join the navy.) Did they live happily ever after? I would never know.

Stacey patted my hand. "It's okay, Mary Anne," she said with a gentle smile. Like all my friends, she knows how emotional I am and how easily I cry. But she couldn't have known how connected I felt to that boy in the picture.

Mal, meanwhile, had whipped out the mystery notebook again. "L. S., right?" she asked Stacey. "And H. I. W.?" She jotted down the initials on a fresh page. "Now, how are we going to figure out what those initials stand for?"

"Laura Stern," said Kristy, "and Henry Isaiah Williams."

"Whoa!" said Abby. "That was quick. How did you know?"

Kristy shrugged. "I don't know. I made those names up. There must be plenty of people with those initials. But how do we know the box is even connected to our mystery?"

We were silent for a moment. "Also," said Mal, "how do we know the letters are initials? They might stand for something else, you know?"

"Maybe this box is what everyone is looking for," said Stacey. "Maybe it's really valuable or something."

As you can tell, it doesn't take long for the BSC members to switch into detective mode. Present us with a mystery and we plunge right in. Part of me, though, didn't want this mystery to be BSC property. I felt possessive about my sailor boy, and I wanted very much to be the one to find out who he was. So I have to admit I was glad when Claudia's digital clock flipped over to six and our meeting officially ended. Everyone had to head home for dinner, and there'd be no more talk that night about L. S. and H. I. W. and who they might be.

"Two mysteries!" Kristy said as we were leaving the Kishis' house. "We'll have to work twice as hard to solve them both." She was practically rubbing her hands in anticipation.

I thought of the music box nestled carefully inside my backpack. If I had my way, I'd be the one to solve its mystery.

Back at home, the first thing I did was take the music box upstairs and place it carefully on my dresser. I opened it and listened to the song one more time while I looked at the picture and the letter. *Twinkle, twinkle little star, how I wonder what you are.* Finding the secret compartment seemed like a big step along my way to unraveling the mystery. But what was the next step? Figuring that out would take some thought.

I closed the box and headed downstairs. I was suddenly very hungry, and I was hoping Sharon had made something good for dinner. But when I walked into the kitchen, I found out that dinner was the farthest thing from her mind. She was sitting at the kitchen table, looking dazed. The table was overflowing with piles of letters and photos and papers.

"Wow," I said. "What's all this?"

"Granny and Pop-Pop's papers," said Sharon wearily. "I've been sorting them."

"I didn't realize there'd be so much stuff," I said. "I thought it was just letters."

"This isn't even all of it," Sharon answered, gesturing to the floor next to the table, where three cardboard boxes waited to be opened.

"It's a lot more than letters. There's two life-times worth of memories here," she said with a little smile. "I guess I can't expect to organize it in one afternoon."

I pulled up a chair and sat down. "Have you found anything interesting?" I asked.

"Oh, tons," said Sharon. "I mean, there's a lot of boring junk, like bank statements and electric bills. But I've also found things like Granny's third-grade class picture, and Pop-Pop's prize-winning essay on what it means to be an American. He wrote that when he was eleven." Sharon sounded less tired now, and her eyes were sparkling as she talked.

"Cool," I said. "I bet he'll be glad to see that again. It's probably been buried in that drawer for years."

"I think they're both happy I've taken this project on," said Sharon. "They seemed very enthusiastic when I asked for permission to sort their papers. I hope they'll like the scrap-book. I'm just going to choose a few special things for that." She picked up a letter from the top of the closest pile. "This, for example. It's a letter Pop-Pop wrote to Granny while he was in basic training in the army." She put that down and picked up a picture. "And this has to go in, too. Can you believe how pretty Granny was as a little girl?"

"I love those ringlets," I said. "This is great.

But it looks like a huge job. Do you really think you can finish by the time their cruise is over?"

Sharon sighed. "I hope so. Are you still willing to help?"

"Definitely. Just tell me what you want me to do."

"I thought you might be interested in these," she said, picking up a thick stack of envelopes tied with a piece of string. "They're letters Granny wrote to her cousin June, back when they were both just about your age."

"Neat," I said. "I'd love to read them. But if Granny wrote them, how did they end up back at her house?"

"June died a few years ago," said Sharon. "I guess her family sent these along when they were cleaning out her house."

I looked at the stack of letters and felt a shiver of excitement. It would be like a living history lesson to read through them. I'd learn what it was like to be a young girl growing up in Stoneybrook over fifty years ago!

Sharon and I talked for awhile longer, until we realized we'd better clear off the table and fix something for dinner. By the time my dad came home, we'd pulled together a quick meal. After supper, Dawn called. She and I must have talked for nearly an hour, since I had to fill her in on everything that was happening: the flood, the mystery at Granny and Pop-

Pop's, and, most especially, the news about the music box. I even came close to telling her about the dreams I'd been having and why the boy in the picture looked so familiar to me, but I stopped short. I just wasn't ready to share that with anyone. Dawn was fascinated by the mysteries and disappointed to have left Stoneybrook before they came to light.

By the time we finished talking, it was late. I was suddenly very, very tired. It had been a long day. I took one of Granny's letters to bed with me, but I was barely able to glance at it before my eyes fell shut.

Still, what I read gave me a little chill. In handwriting that was somehow familiar, even though it didn't look like Granny's current style, the young Granny was promising to fill June in on "all the goings-on next door." As I drifted off to sleep, I couldn't help wondering if "next door" could possibly refer to the house that now belongs to Granny and Pop-Pop. If so, maybe the letters sitting so neatly in a stack on my desk would hold some clue to one — or both! — of the mysteries I was hoping to solve.

CHAPTER 9

Friday

Whoa! Major miscalculation. I hate to tell you, Abby, but your hero Eddie made a bodacious boo-boo.

It could happen to anywon. I know it culd sure hapen to me!

Other than that, though, Eddie seems okay. He sure didn't give us any cause for suspicion.

But thats exacly why hes a majore suspekt! Dont you see?

I guess we should finish this discussion in the mystery notebook. Meanwhile, here's what happened over at the Barrett-DeWitts'...

Stacey and Claudia arrived at the Barrett-DeWitt house on Friday morning prepared for two things: construction and detection. They knew all about the playhouse the kids were building. Stacey and Claud were excited about helping out. They'd each brought a hammer so they could "bang nails," as Claud put it. Claudia had also brought a monkey wrench, two screwdrivers, and her eyelash curler. The wrench and screwdrivers had come from her dad's toolbox; the eyelash curler was Claudia's. "You never know what tools you might need," she explained.

Stacey and Claudia had dressed for the occasion, as only the two of them can. Stacey was wearing a pair of pink denim overall shorts with a white baby T underneath. Purple Doc Martens and a white baseball cap — with her ponytail pulled through the back — completed the look.

Claudia had on her favorite painter's pants. They used to be white, but she's worn them during so many art projects that they are now splattered with paint in every color of the rainbow. To complement the pants, Claudia wore a tie-dyed shirt she made herself that features a huge yellow peace sign surrounded by starbursts of orange, red, and purple. She also had on her red high-top sneakers, and she had braided her hair in two pigtails, tied with purple ribbons, to keep it tidy and out of the way.

As far as preparations for spying went, they were simple. Stacey had brought along the mystery notebook, and she and Claudia had talked over their plans. They'd decided, after hearing what Kristy and I had said at Wednesday's BSC meeting, that it wouldn't be a bad idea to keep a close eye on Eddie and Jim and their crews. After all, they'd reasoned, maybe Eddie and Jim acted suspiciously *all* the time. Maybe they were just nosy guys who liked to poke around in their clients' houses. Maybe their odd behavior at Granny and Pop-Pop's house didn't mean anything at all.

In any case, Claudia and Stacey agreed that it was important to watch both men and their crews carefully.

Of course, that didn't turn out to be so easy. Why? Because they also had the Barretts and the DeWitts to watch.

Fortunately, some of the younger kids had become bored with measuring and hammering. Lindsay had organized them into a "decorating committee," and they were very busy drawing pictures and making cardboard frames for them so that the playhouse would have "art." They were also making curtains as well as placemats, tablecloths, and anything else they could think of in the way of home furnishings.

Mrs. DeWitt was home and willing to keep an eye on the younger kids. They were in the playroom, where she could check up on them every so often. That left Claudia and Stacey free to supervise the older kids as they worked on the playhouse.

"You go out and check on the playhouse," Stacey whispered to Claudia, soon after they'd arrived. "I'll pretend I have to use the bathroom first. That way I can see what Eddie and Jim and everyone are up to."

While Claudia went out to the shed in the backyard, where the playhouse was being assembled, Stacey headed upstairs. She tiptoed past the bathroom and peered through the doorway that led into the new addition. There was no sign of Jim or Eddie or any of their helpers. Stacey raised an eyebrow. Where were they all? Out snooping?

Then she heard the murmur of voices coming from one of the rooms near the back of the addition. As silently as possible, she moved down the hall toward the sound. The voices grew louder. Stacey peeked around the corner carefully.

But not carefully enough.

"Hey, good morning," said Eddie cheerfully.

He and Jake and Lori, along with Jim and Dooley, were sitting in a circle on the floor in the middle of a nearly finished room. An open box of doughnuts sat in the middle of the circle, and Eddie and the other workers were sipping from large containers of coffee. "You must be looking for that wild bunch of maniacs known as the children of the house." He grinned at her and held up a chocolate-covered doughnut. "You're just in time for coffee break. Care for a cruller?"

Stacey blushed. How could she admit, even to herself, that she'd been planning to spy on this perfectly nice man? "Thanks, but I just had breakfast," she said. "I'm Stacey, and you're right, I'm here to baby-sit. Do you know where the kids are?" she asked, even though she knew the kids were out in the shed.

"They're busy building. Those kids sure have a knack for construction," he added, smiling and shaking his head. "Didn't take much to fire them up about building their own playhouse. They're out there hammering away every day, rain or shine." He stood up and brushed off his pants. Then he led Stacey to a window in the back of the room. "They're out in that shed," he said, pointing.

"Oh, great. Thanks." Stacey headed out of the room, feeling mortified. Eddie was so nice. How could he be up to anything wrong?

"That's just it," Claudia whispered when Stacey had joined her in the shed and filled her in on what Eddie and the other workers were doing. "Of course he would act like a nice guy. I'll go check them out a little later. Meanwhile," she added, raising her voice slightly, "look at what these kids have done!"

Stacey stepped back to take it all in. The playhouse was a small building that looked very much like a miniature version of the Barrett-DeWitt house. It had four windows, including two tiny ones on either side of the door. There was a peaked roof, covered in gray shingles like the ones on the real house. Stacey thought it looked great, even though some of the shingles were crooked, the door was so low that only Suzi could go through it without ducking, and the whole house seemed to lean a bit to the right. "Very impressive," she said. "You guys have really worked hard. I love the little windows."

"I did those!" cried Buddy. "See how I nailed them in really good?"

"Really *well*," Stacey said, correcting him absently as she checked out Buddy's work. Sure enough, he'd nailed the windows in well. So well that they'd probably never budge, even in a hurricane. Even in a tornado, thought Stacey, smiling to herself as she looked at the dozens of nails clustered around each window frame.

"Great job," she told Buddy. "And who put the roof on?"

"We did," said Buddy. "Lindsay held the shingles and I hammered. Eddie showed us how."

"It sounds like Eddie has helped a lot," said Stacey with a meaningful glance at Claudia.

"He has," said Lindsey. "Every morning when we come out here there's a pile of wood all cut to the right size so all we have to do is start hammering. And he checks on us all the time to make sure we're on the right track." Lindsey picked up a hammer and reached for a nail in the carpenter's apron tied around her waist. "I'm going to finish off some of the work inside," she announced. Then she pulled the door open and ducked low to fit through it.

"It looks as if you're almost done," Stacey said. "When is the housewarming party?" She was joking, but Buddy took her seriously.

"That's a great idea," he said. "We could have a party for this house at the same time as the one for the new addition. Mom and Franklin were planning to invite all their friends over for a barbecue next week. We can invite our friends, too, and show off the play-house!"

"Yea!" shouted Taylor. "Let's go ask right now. I bet Mom will say yes."

"When you go in," called Lindsey from inside the playhouse, "ask Eddie if he can come out soon. The playhouse is pretty much done, and we need his help to move it outside."

"I'll go with you guys," Claudia said in a hurry. This was her chance to spy on Eddie and the other workers. She followed Buddy and Taylor as they ran into the house. And while they went into the living room to find Mrs. De-Witt, Claudia headed upstairs.

There was no need to tiptoe, since Claudia could hear hammering and sawing coming from the addition. Nobody could hear her coming, even if they tried, over that racket. Still, Claudia proceeded slowly, hoping to catch Eddie or one of the other workers where he didn't belong.

No such luck.

Eddie was using a screw gun to attach some wallboard. Jake was hammering on window trim. Lori was measuring a piece of molding. And Jim and Dooley were both halfway under the sink in the new bathroom, attaching some pipes.

Claudia tried not to feel disappointed. After all, finding everyone at their jobs instead of snooping around seemed to prove that the snooping they were doing at Granny and Pop-Pop's was out of the ordinary. Didn't it?

"Excuse me," she said to Eddie. "I can tell you're really busy, but the kids wanted to know if you could come down and help them move the playhouse out into the yard. When you have a chance."

"When I have a chance!" said Eddie. "Hey, if that building's ready to move, I'm ready to move it." He looked as excited as a little kid on Christmas morning. "I can't wait to see how it looks in the spot we've chosen for it."

Eddie and the other workers took a break and came out to the shed. Inside, they oohed and aahed over the playhouse and told the kids what a terrific job they'd done. Then they rolled up their sleeves and prepared to move the playhouse.

There was only one tiny problem.

It wouldn't fit through the door.

CHAPTER 10

That same Friday, while Stacey and Claudia were doing construction over at the Barrett-DeWitts', I was doing some construction of my own. I wasn't building a house, though. I was building knowledge, about events of the past that might have very much to do with my present life.

I'd woken late, with the sun shining full strength through my window. I must have been even more tired than I'd realized.

As I rubbed my eyes and yawned, I felt a little shiver of excitement. You know that feeling when you first wake up on Christmas morning or on your birthday? You're not even fully conscious yet, but somehow you know the day's going to bring wonderful things your way. Surprises, all wrapped up in colorful paper, just for you. Well, that's how I felt as I stretched — and I didn't even know why. Until I opened my eyes. Then, suddenly, it all came back. Right away, I saw the stack of letters sitting on my desk. That was the wonderful thing, the thing I couldn't wait to "unwrap."

The second thing I saw was a note from Sharon. She must have tiptoed in early that morning to prop it up on my dresser. "Dear Mary Anne," it said. "I really appreciate how hard you've been working over at Granny and Pop-Pop's. I think you deserve a day off. There's plenty to eat in the fridge, and it looks like a nice day for a swim or a bike ride. Enjoy! I'll see you tonight. Love, Sharon."

Do I have the nicest stepmom in the world or what?

I stretched again, yawned some more, and slowly climbed out of bed. There was no need to hurry. I could spend the whole day in whatever way I wanted. And I knew exactly what I was going to do. I wasn't interested in going to the pool or riding my bike.

I was interested in reading those letters.

First, though, I headed downstairs to find myself some breakfast. The house was quiet and peaceful, and I hummed contentedly as I set out cereal, milk, and juice. I took my time eating and washing up. Afterward I went back upstairs and put on shorts and a T-shirt. Then, bringing the letters, a bottle of water, and a pillow with me, I headed out to the hammock in the backyard, ready to settle in for the rest of the morning. The hammock is tied between two young maple trees, and there's no more comfortable place to lie in the dappled shade of a summer day.

I began to read. At first, I hunted everywhere for more mentions of the "goings-on next door," and for clues about the mysteries I was trying to solve. Slowly, though, I began to forget about that and to enjoy learning what Granny had been like as a girl my age. First of all, her name was not, of course, Granny. It was Grace. From the letters I discovered that Grace had had curly blonde hair (I remembered the ringlets I'd seen in the picture Sharon had shown me) that she longed to cut into a more fashionable style. She had a white kitten named Smidge. She had never kissed a boy. She wished she'd had a little brother.

As I read, I also discovered that Grace was interested in the same kinds of things I am:

Dear June, Smidge did the funniest thing yesterday...

She had the same kinds of concerns:

Dear June, Why can't parents understand that a girl my age can be trusted to make her own decisions?

And she seemed to have just as many good friends as I do:

Dear June, Wait until you hear about what Maisie and Beth and I are going to do tomorrow....

I began to piece together the situation. Until that summer, June and her parents had lived three doors from Grace and her parents. (June's mother and Grace's mother were sisters and very close.) Then June's father had developed terrible allergies, and the doctors had ordered him to live in a drier climate. Within weeks, June's family had packed up and moved to Arizona!

The cousins missed each other desperately, that was obvious. But it was also clear that they were maintaining a very close relationship by writing regularly. In some ways, their friendship reminded me of mine and Dawn's. Like June and Grace, we're family as well as friends, and while we live far from each other now, we do our best to stay in touch — although we're more likely to pick up the phone. Those long-ago girls wouldn't have dreamed of running up the kind of phone bills we're used to!

Lying there in the hammock, swaying gently and enjoying the slight breeze as I read through the letters, I began to feel as if Grace were a friend herself, someone I would have known and liked if we had been girls at the same time. I became so involved in learning about her that I nearly forgot all about those "goings-on next door." Then I came across a letter that made me sit up in the hammock, so suddenly that I nearly tipped over.

Dear Cousin June,

You won't believe what happened over at the Bailey's last night. Remember how I told you about Lydia's latest beau, Johnny Buckman, and how handsome he is? Well, it turns out that Mr. Bailey is not nearly as impressed as I am with his daughter's suitor's looks. In fact, he's not impressed period. Quite the opposite. He's been fairly clear about that. Loud and clear. The whole neighborhood knows how he feels....

As I read that letter and the next and the next, I began to figure out that the Baileys were the family living in the house next door, the one that now belongs to Granny and Pop-Pop. Lydia was the teenage daughter. I guessed she must be about nineteen. And Mr. Bailey, her father, sounded as if he could be in the *Guinness Book of World Records* under "Strictest Father."

Lydia was beautiful, with long dark hair and green eyes. (Grace envied those eyes and often told June so.) She always had boyfriends, and before June moved away, she and Grace kept tabs on which ones were cutest, which ones were sweetest, and how long each one lasted. In one letter, Grace reminded June about Sam Tolliver, who'd only had half a date with Lydia. (She'd dumped him before the movie even started. Grace and June, who'd followed them to the picture show, had seen the whole thing). Sam still held the record for shortest romance.

Now, according to Grace, Johnny Buckman was a sure bet for winning the longest romance category. *I think Lydia's really stuck on him,* wrote Grace.

And I don't blame her one bit. Those dark blue eyes of his, that sweet smile... Oh, my heart skips a beat just thinking of him.

But, as usual, Mr. Bailey didn't approve. And he wasn't shy about letting Lydia know. He didn't like Johnny Buckman. He didn't think Johnny Buckman was good enough for his daughter. And he'd forbidden Johnny Buckman to come anywhere near her.

But Johnny Buckman seemed to be just as "stuck on" Lydia as she was on him. He wouldn't or couldn't stay away. And every time Mr. Bailey caught Johnny and Lydia together, he threw such a fit that everybody on the block could hear him.

Last night I woke up around midnight because I heard something outside. I looked out the window and what do you think I saw? Lydia was sneaking out her kitchen door. Johnny was just behind their garage. I saw him in the moonlight.

It was no wonder that Grace was fascinated by Lydia and Johnny's romance. I would have been, too. After all, they were "star-crossed lovers," just like Romeo and Juliet. She was beautiful, he was handsome, and they were forbidden to meet. How romantic!

Grace told June every detail. She wrote about the notes Lydia tossed out her window to Johnny, about the flowers Johnny tossed back to Lydia. She wrote about how Johnny would hang around in the bushes, waiting for Mr. Bailey to go to sleep, and then throw pebbles at Lydia's window until she appeared, smiling down at him. Grace saw it all.

Grace also had an ear out for other news June might find interesting.

It's not as if Mr. Bailey is perfect either, she wrote in one letter.

In fact, he's in big, big trouble right now. Papa read it in the paper last night. Do you remember that Mr. Bailey is president of the First National Bank of Stoneybrook? Well, not anymore. It seems he was caught stealing money from the bank!

Mr. Bailey's legal difficulties didn't seem to affect the way Johnny felt about Lydia. The romance continued, and while Mr. Bailey still objected to it, Grace wrote that she noticed fewer "fits". *I suppose other things are weighing more heavily on his mind,* she told June.

By this time, I was reading through the letters as quickly as I could. It was like reading a novel that came in installments. I couldn't wait to see what happened next.

As it turned out, what happened next was very, very interesting.

Dear June, the most mysterious thing happened last night. I went to bed early, so I didn't see any of Johnny and Lydia's comings and goings. But then, in the middle of the night, something woke me up. A sound. A strange, scraping sound. As I lay in bed listening to it, I became very curious. The sound continued. Finally, I couldn't stand the suspense anymore, and I jumped up and peeked out of my window. They were burying something.

I put down the letter. My heart was racing. Quickly, I pawed through the other letters, hoping to discover that Grace had found out who was in the backyard and what they were burying. But there were no further mentions of the episode. In fact, Grace soon seemed to have tired of writing about the Baileys. Instead, she began to exclaim over the "handsome fellow" she'd met at the ice-cream shop. Any other time, I might have loved reading about a new romance. But at the moment, I had other things on my mind.

The letters had made me think — hard. And I was beginning to put two and two together. Not about the backyard burial. The answer to that was fairly plain to me. I was pretty sure it was Mr. Bailey, hiding away some of the money he'd stolen from the bank. That seemed obvious, and I was looking forward to telling my friends about it at the BSC meeting that afternoon. It might explain why people were so interested in the backyard of Granny and Pop-Pop's house.

But what I was really interested in was this: Suppose you had a secret boyfriend, one your father disapproved of. A boyfriend with deep blue eyes and a special smile. And suppose that boyfriend gave you a wonderful, romantic present. What would you do with it? Would you keep it in your room? Absolutely not. You'd hide it away somewhere, where you knew it would be safe.

I was fairly certain that the music box had been a gift from Johnny to Lydia.

CHAPTER 11

That afternoon, at the BSC meeting, I couldn't wait to tell my friends about Granny's letters. So as soon as Stacey and Claudia finished telling us about the latest developments at the Barrett-DeWitts', I started in. I explained about June and Grace. I told them about Johnny and Lydia and their forbidden romance. And I told them about Mr. Bailey and his embezzling.

The interesting thing was the way my friends reacted. I'd assumed that, like me, everybody would be overcome by the romance of the story. And Mal and Claudia certainly were. They loved hearing about Johnny and Lydia, and they were more interested than ever in finding out the truth behind the music box mystery. But Kristy saw the letters in a different light, and so did Abby. To them, the letters had more to do with the other mystery at Granny and Pop-Pop's. They were very excited by the fact that Granny had seen someone burying something in *that* backyard. Jessi and Stacey, meanwhile, were becoming convinced that the mysteries were intertwined, and that by solving one we could solve them both.

"Isn't it romantic?" I asked, after I finished the story. I sighed. "I wonder what ever happened with Johnny and Lydia."

"And I wonder what ever happened with Lydia's father," said Kristy, tapping her pencil thoughtfully on Claudia's desk. "And the money he stole."

I should have known she wouldn't be caught up in the romance of the situation. I ignored her. Somehow I couldn't work up a whole lot of excitement over some money that had probably been found ages ago, though I guess if there *were* money in their backyard, Granny and Pop-Pop might like to know about it. "If only there was some way we could be positive the music box was a gift from Johnny," I said. "I'd really like to know." I thought of my sad-eyed sailor. Privately, I'd already begun thinking of him as Johnny.

"I'm not so sure the music box has anything to do with Johnny and Lydia," said Mal. She was flipping through some of the notes she'd made in the mystery notebook. "I mean, what about H. I. W. and L. S.? The only initial that matches up at all is the L. How do you explain that?"

"I can't," I said. "But I still think the box was a gift from Johnny." How could I tell my friends that I was basing my guess on the fact that both Johnny and the boy in my dreams had deep blue eyes? They'd think I'd gone off my rocker.

"I think we need to do some more research into the other people who've lived in that house," said Jessi. "Who knows what we might find out? That music box could have been hidden there way before Lydia and her family moved in. And we might find out something about the so-called treasure in the back-yard — like, that somebody's already dug it up."

"I'll help you," said Stacey, who was nodding in agreement.

"I'm going to spend some time scouting around in that yard," vowed Abby. "We can't dig there now, obviously, since it would draw too much attention. But as soon as we have the chance, I'm dying to start shoveling. I bet the treasure's still there and my guess is that's what everybody's looking for." Abby was, as usual, ready for action.

"Can I see that photograph again?" asked Claudia. Her thoughts were still on the music box mystery.

I'd brought all the "evidence" — the letters, the note from H. I. W. to L. S., and the photo —

to the meeting with me. I handed over the photo.

Claudia looked at it closely, frowning a little. "If you'll let me borrow this, I may be able to blow it up and see if any clues surface."

Reluctantly, since it was my only picture of the boy I'd come to think of as Johnny, I agreed that she could take it, just for a night.

By the end of our meeting, it was pretty clear that each of us was committed to doing what we could toward solving one — or both — of the mysteries we'd become involved in. And over the next few days, everyone did a lot of investigating.

Sunday

My eyes are bleary. My hands smell like chemicals. And my feet are sore from standing in the darkroom all day. It would be worth it if I could say I proved something . . . but I can't.

Claudia's entry in the mystery notebook revealed her frustration. She'd been so sure she could find some clues in that photograph. Clues that would lead us to the true identity of H. I. W. and L. S.

Claudia, I should mention, is an artist in the darkroom. She's taken some photography classes and learned how to shoot pictures, develop the film, and print photos. She's so good that she even used her skills once before to help solve a mystery. That's why she thought she could do it again this time.

She worked as fast as she could, since she knew I wouldn't feel entirely comfortable until that picture was back in my hands. First, she examined it closely with a tool called a loupe, which is a special magnifying glass for looking at pictures or negatives. She was hoping to be able to see something not visible to the naked eye. (Isn't that a strange expression? As if our eyes usually go around dressed in their Sunday best.) Something like a name, etched on that ID bracelet.

No such luck.

But Claudia went ahead with her plan anyway. First she took a picture of the picture. Then she developed the film and began to print and enlarge, print and enlarge, until she'd blown up every section of that picture to nearly life-size.

She brought the prints over to show me that night when she returned the original photo. We pored over them. I felt a secret thrill when I saw the boy's eyes. They were my sailor's eyes, no doubt about it. But was my sailor named Johnny, and had he dated a girl named Lydia? The photos gave me no sign. The ID bracelet had no trace of a name on it. Instead, there were a bunch of stars engraved on the place where a name would usually be. They were pretty, but they didn't tell us a thing about the identity of the owner of the bracelet. Claudia had hit a dead end.

Monday

Claudia, if you think your eyes are bleary, you should try reading through hundreds of pages of tiny, tiny print, looking for five little letters ——

Or hunting through file upon file searching for a certain address ——

That's right, Claudia, you got off easily. At least in your darkroom you don't have to deal with a certain Ms. Stephowski. . . .

Stacey, Jessi, and Mal spent Monday afternoon at Stoneybrook Town Hall, searching for answers.

Stacey and Jessi were interested in finding out about the history of Granny and Pop-Pop's house. They wanted to leave with a complete list of everyone who'd lived there since it was built.

And Mal was planning to go over the old town voter rolls, looking for every single person she could find with the initials L .S. or H. I. W.

But first they had to face the dragon: Ms. Stepkowski.

"Can I help you girls?" she asked, looking over her half glasses. She stood on one side of the counter, and the three of them stood on the other. Mal was convinced that Ms. Stepkowski was standing on a box because she seemed so imposing. But Stacey said it was just her attitude that made them feel like little kids.

"We need to look at some records," said Jessi.

"We've done it before, and we know how," said Mal. That was true. We'd done detective work at Town Hall before, and nobody had ever given us a hard time about it.

"We don't need to bother you at all," added Stacey helpfully.

But Ms. Stepkowski seemed bothered anyway. Mal said it was as if the records were her personal property, she was that reluctant to part with them. However, the town records are open to the public. Ms. Stepkowski sat Mal, Jessi, and Stacey down in an empty room where the town council meets in the evenings. Then, box by box, she brought in the files, refusing help.

When she'd set the last box on the table and left, Mal and Jessi and Stacey looked at each other and burst into giggles. Ms. Stepkowski poked her head in the door and glared at them. They stifled their laughter, then settled down to work.

It wasn't fun, especially with Ms. Stepkowski stopping in every fifteen minutes to check on them, but they were able to accomplish what they'd come for. By the end of the afternoon, Jessi and Stacey had an accurate list of the owners of the house. Three families had lived there before the Baileys moved in, and one single woman had lived there for a time between the Baileys and Granny and Pop-Pop. The next step would be to do some detective work on each of those families.

None of the previous owners had the initials L. S., but Mal was able to search out a dozen other Stoneybrookites who did. H. I. W. posed a tougher problem. There were only three leads for that name.

Finally, Stacey told Ms. Stepkowski they were done and offered to help her take the boxes back to the record room. She refused her help and shooed my friends out the door.

Out on the front steps of Town Hall, Mal began to laugh.

"What is it?" asked Stacey.

Mal couldn't speak for a second. Then, finally, she told them what was so funny. As they were leaving, she'd caught a glimpse of Ms. Stepkowski's name tag. "Her first name is

Laura!" Mal said. "Can you imagine? Our mysterious L. S. might have been staring us right in the face the whole time!"

Tuesday
The records don't lie. I'm positively, absolutely sure that the money is still there. And when we dig it up, you can bet it'll be big news....

Kristy was off in another direction, checking through microfilmed copies of the *Stoneybrook News* at the library. She was trying to learn whether the money Mr. Bailey had embezzled had ever turned up, and what she found convinced her that it hadn't. Here's what she found: Nothing. Zip. Zero. (That's how she put it anyway.) To her, that was conclusive evidence that the money was still out there. And she and Abby agreed on the best way to find it.

Wednesday
Well, there's no question about it. Certain people—Kristy and I included—are convinced that there's treasure in the backyard. If we want to be the ones

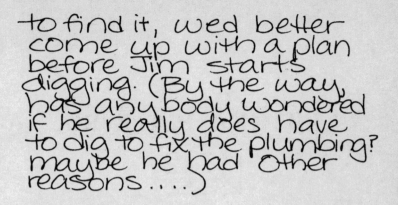

to find it, we'd better come up with a plan before Jim starts digging. (By the way, has anybody wondered if he really does have to dig to fix the plumbing? maybe he had other reasons....)

Abby had volunteered to help Sharon at Granny and Pop-Pop's on Wednesday. She worked hard, according to Sharon, but judging from her notes in the mystery notebook, she spied hard, too. And what she saw — Eddie and Jim snooping around, Hank and Esther stopping by to meddle again — convinced her that there was no time to lose. "We have to take action," she said at our meeting that night. "Kristy and I have talked, and we've come up with what we think is a good plan. Want to hear it?"

By that time, I think we were all feeling as if our investigation needed a boost, so we nodded and leaned forward eagerly.

Abby began to fill us in.

CHAPTER 12

"Ready, everyone? Let's do it!"

Kristy was whispering into the huddle we'd made on the sunporch of Granny and Pop-Pop's house. It was Thursday morning, and everyone in the BSC was on hand. I'd explained to Sharon that we had planned a work marathon. With everyone pitching in for one day, we could accomplish a lot. That was true, but we had another motive as well. We were finally going to find out what was so fascinating about that backyard.

Was there really buried treasure? Was it the funds Lydia's father had embezzled? Where was the treasure? Who knew about it, and how did they know? Were our suspicions completely off base?

"Hold on a second," Abby whispered back. "Let me make sure Hank and Esther have arrived." She disappeared into the house for a few seconds. Then she popped back out onto the porch. "They're here," she hissed. "Having doughnuts in the kitchen. And Jim is in there, too. Sharon's not around. I think she's downstairs."

Our plan couldn't miss. We'd scripted and rehearsed our parts. The audience was on hand. Our drama was ready.

"Lights, camera, action!" murmured Kristy. Then, in a louder voice, meant to carry through the screen door all the way into the kitchen, she said, "Wow! You mean you found a box buried in the backyard? How cool!"

"Isn't it?" I asked, trying to make my voice as loud and enthusiastic as possible. "I was just planting some flowers for Granny. And then my shovel hit something metal."

"So what was inside?" asked Jessi.

"Anything interesting?" asked Mal.

"I haven't looked yet," I answered. "I left it where it was. I thought I should show it to Sharon first. After all, this isn't my yard." Did I sound convincing? I hoped so. Kristy was nodding at me encouragingly.

"I think we should look inside it," said Abby. "Isn't the rule 'finders, keepers'?" Abby sounded convincing. That was exactly what she would say — if we really had found a box in the backyard.

Which we hadn't. We were faking it. We wanted to know how certain people would respond to the news that a box had been found. Which people? Well, to be specific, we had figured out that the three people who knew about the supposed buried treasure were Jim Prentice, Hank, and Esther. Hank and Jim had lived in that neighborhood when the Baileys owned the house, and we figured Hank must have told Esther whatever he knew. So we made sure to put on our play at a time when they were all on hand. Hank and Esther had begun to make a habit of stopping by during the mid-morning break, and I happened to know that Jim was scheduled to work that day, so our audience was guaranteed.

"I agree with Abby," Stacey said now, continuing with the script. "I think we should check it out."

"I vote with you two," Claudia put in. "Except for one thing. I think we ought to grab some doughnuts first, to keep up our energy." Claudia had thought of that line, and it was a good one. First of all, because it sounded exactly like something Claudia would say. And second, because it was the perfect way to explain our move into the kitchen, where we could see firsthand how our play was going over.

Claudia's line was our cue to start moving. Kristy began making shooing motions. We trooped into the kitchen, trying to act innocent. As I entered, I took a look around.

The play had worked. There was no question about it.

Jim's eyes were bright with interest. So were Hank's. Esther looked as if she were about to pop.

"Hello, girls," she said. "What's new?"

"Oh, nothing," said Kristy casually.

"Nothing?" asked Esther, arching her eyebrows.

"Nothing," said Kristy.

"What Esther means," Hank said, cutting right to the chase, "is that we just overheard you girls having a very interesting discussion. About something you found in the backyard?"

"Where exactly is it?" asked Jim eagerly. I could tell that he was having a hard time sitting still. He wanted to be in the yard, checking out that box.

"Well . . ." I began, trying to think of what to say next. Obviously our plan had worked. There was no doubt that Hank and Esther and Jim were very, very interested in what we'd found. They'd want to see the box — and the fact was that there wasn't one. I glanced at Kristy, wondering why I hadn't noticed before that this plan wasn't as completely thought out as it could have been. "Umm," I began.

Just then, I was interrupted by a loud, crashing noise coming from the front of the house.

"What the dickens is that?" Hank said, jumping up from his chair.

"It sounds like somebody drove a car into the house," said Jim, following Hank to the front door.

We all ran to see what had happened. Outside, in front of the house, we found three of the metal garbage cans we'd been using rolling around in the driveway. I was curious about who had knocked them over, but Jim and Hank didn't seem to care.

"As long as we're outside, let's go take a look at that box," suggested Jim, leading the way around to the backyard before I could think of any new ways to stall.

As we rounded the corner of the house, I noticed a stooped figure near the rosebushes. "Hey," I said, nudging Kristy. "It's that old man."

"What's he doing here?" she asked. Then she narrowed her eyes and took a better look. "He's *digging*, that's what," she said.

As we came closer to the man, I heard Jim gasp.

"Dad?" he said suddenly.

"Dad?" Kristy whispered to me, raising her eyebrows. So the old man was Jim Prentice's father. Interesting.

108

The man looked up. "Oops," he said when he saw the crowd descending upon him.

"Dad, what are you doing?" asked Jim.

"Same thing all of you have been doing," the man said shortly. "Looking for treasure." He nodded at me. "You're related to the people who live here now, aren't you?"

"Sort of," I said.

"That's how you knew about the Bailey money, then," he said. "I overheard you saying you thought there was a box down here. Well, where is it?" He sounded impatient. I realized that he was probably the one who'd knocked over the trash cans to create enough of a diversion so that he could look for the box himself.

"Hold on, hold on," said Hank. "You know about the Bailey money?" he asked.

"Sure," said the old man. "I lived across the street when old man Bailey embezzled those funds. I'll never forget it. Everyone assumed that he'd buried the money, since it was never found."

"Exactly," said Hank. "I remember hearing the same rumors."

Jim nodded. "Everyone in the neighborhood knew about it."

"And now these girls have found the money," said Esther. "Isn't that something?"

Hank and Jim didn't look too happy about that. Neither did Jim's dad.

"Well," I said, clearing my throat nervously, "actually, to tell the truth, we didn't really find the money. We, um, didn't even find a box. We were just sort of playing a game." I knew my explanation sounded pretty lame, but it was the best I could come up with on short notice.

"A game?" asked Jim. He shook his head sadly.

Hank looked peeved.

But Mr. Prentice didn't seem fazed by the news. "Well, in that case," he said, "I suggest we do some digging. I've been scouting this yard and doing a lot of thinking, and I have an idea that I know exactly where old Bailey buried the goods." He led us to a spot at the foot of a crabapple tree. "This tree would have been planted right around that time," he said. "I bet he did it to cover his tracks."

Jim grabbed a shovel that had been leaning against a fence and without any further discussion began to dig. He seemed to have complete faith in his father's theory.

The rest of us stood around and watched. I wanted to point out that the backyard — and anything in it — actually belonged to Granny and Pop-Pop, but I was too shy to speak up. Sharon had come up from the basement by that time (she hadn't even heard the crashing noise from outside) and I filled her in on what was happening. It took her awhile to understand the truth — that she was apparently the only one who didn't know that buried treasure might lie in her parents' backyard.

"Well, how about that," she said. "I wonder if Granny and Pop-Pop know. It'll be fun to find out if anything's really there. I guess Jim was going to have to dig up the yard anyway."

I thought of Grace's letter to June, about the mysterious sounds in the backyard one night. "I think Granny might have known a long time ago," I said, "but maybe she's forgotten." I watched Jim dig for awhile. I still couldn't manage to feel excited about a box full of money. I was hoping that the "treasure" would turn out to be something from the past, some evidence that would prove once and for all that Johnny and Lydia were the L. S. and H. I. W.

Jim was digging hard and fast, and working up a sweat. Hank stood over him, offering suggestions, while old Mr. Prentice supervised. I was beginning to doubt that Jim would find anything when suddenly we all heard it.

Clunk.

The shovel had hit something that wasn't just dirt. Jim tried the same spot again. There was another clunk. He tossed the shovel aside and hunkered down, using his bare hands to claw dirt away, so that he could see what he'd hit. "It's a box!" he crowed. "A gray metal box." He scrabbled away some more, and soon he'd freed the box from its grave. He pulled it out — it was about the size of a typewriter case — and brought it to the porch steps.

We all gathered around him; my friends and I, Hank and Esther, Sharon and old Mr. Prentice. I held my breath as Jim tried the latches. I didn't hear anyone else breathing, either.

The box wasn't locked. The hinges gave a rusty squeal as Jim pried the lid open. We all leaned forward to peek inside.

Jim sneezed as he rummaged around inside the box, and a cloud of mildew-smelling dust rose up. "Let's see," he said. "The first layer just looks like papers. Deeds and such."

Old Mr. Prentice looked as if he wanted to snatch the box out of his son's hands. "What's underneath?" he asked impatiently. "Where's the money?"

Jim rummaged some more. Then he looked up and smiled. "I hate to say it," he said, "but there isn't a cent in here. Just more papers. They must have meant something to old Bailey, but they're worthless to us. I think the story of the buried treasure was just that. A story. There never *was* any money."

Old Mr. Prentice tightened his lips and made a harrumphing sound. Hank said something under his breath that I didn't quite catch. Esther looked disappointed, and so did Kristy and the rest of my friends.

I was disappointed, too. But not about the money. I was disappointed because, even though we'd found a buried box, nothing in it had told us anything about the beautiful music box and its history.

CHAPTER 13

Friday

What a great party! I have a feeling that the Barrett-DeWitt family is going to be very, very happy in that house for many years to come....

"Welcome, welcome, come on in!" Buddy was at the door, beaming as he greeted us. It was Friday, and my friends and I had headed straight from our BSC meeting to the Barrett-DeWitts', where the addition-warming bash was already well under way. We'd been invited as guests, not as sitters. I'd been concerned about how the Barrett-DeWitt kids had handled their disappointment over the playhouse, but Buddy seemed to have forgotten about it.

The house was decorated with balloons and streamers, and Buddy was dressed in his good clothes. Music was playing, and a long table in the dining room was covered with food the guests had brought. Kids were running around. I spotted Claire Pike and Suzi as they dashed through the living room, and I noticed Charlotte and Lindsey sitting together on a bench, munching on chips. Parents were gathered in little groups, holding paper plates as they ate and talked. I saw Mrs. Kuhn chatting with Dr. Johanssen. Eddie and Lori and the other crew members were there, too, checking out the food.

"It's a party," declared Claud with satisfaction as she eyed the chips and dips. She started toward the table.

"Don't you want the tour?" asked Buddy. "We're giving tours of the addition every ten

115

minutes." He made a show of checking his watch. "And, as a matter of fact, there's one leaving right now!"

How could we resist? "We're ready when you are," I said. "Lead the way."

Buddy took us upstairs. "The boys' room is the coolest," he said. "Do you want to see it first?"

"Let's save it," said Abby, humoring Buddy. "I always like to save the best for last."

Buddy grinned. "Cool," he said. "In that case, I'll start with the bathrooms." He led us toward the first door on the right. "Ta-da!" he said, showing us the inside. I saw a nice large bathtub plus a shower stall. Fluffy new blue towels hung on the racks. "This is for the whole family to use," Buddy said. Then he led us down the hall. "And this one," he said, showing us another, smaller bathroom, "is just for us kids."

From the beginning, the Barrett-DeWitt family had planned for their addition to include two bathrooms. (In fact, Kristy remembers Suzi suggesting that they have "a bazillion bathrooms." You can't have too many bathrooms when you have a big family.)

"I like this bathroom," said Jessi, looking around at the gleaming new fixtures, the green towels, and the jungle-animal wallpaper. "It feels like you're in the rain forest."

"That was Lindsey's idea," said Buddy. "Isn't it great?"

What was great, I thought, was how well a bunch of kids from two different families had learned to get along. I remembered how many squabbles the kids used to have when the families first blended. That all came to an end soon after they'd moved into this house, though. At first, the fact that the house was so tiny had led to even more squabbles. The kids would fight family against family or girls against the boys. It never seemed to end. But then the kids pulled together for a common goal: Small as it was, they loved their new house, and they wanted to make sure their parents wouldn't decide to move because of the cramped quarters. They felt so strongly about it that once they actually staged a picket line with signs and all!

That's when Mr. and Mrs. DeWitt informed the kids that they had no intention of moving, and that they planned to build an addition instead. The plans they had drawn up showed a bunch of small bedrooms so that each of the children could have their own space. (Even little Marnie and Ryan needed their own rooms. Marnie is a restless sleeper, and when she and Ryan were in a room together she frequently woke him up, which in turn would keep their parents up.)

But, at the groundbreaking party, the older kids made an announcement. They didn't *want* a whole bunch of little rooms. They wanted two giant ones, one for the three older girls and one for the two older boys. That's how close the new siblings had become.

Now that the addition was finished, the older kids had their dorm-style rooms. And Marnie and Ryan each had a small room of their own. The idea was that by the time the toddlers were old enough to want to share rooms, the oldest kids might want to have rooms of their own and they could switch. Meanwhile, the tiny room that the girls had been sharing before the addition was built would become a place the kids could use for quiet time, and the room in the basement that the boys had been using would become a play area.

The house that had once been so cramped and overflowing had become a palace. And if Buddy was any indication, the kids were thrilled with the addition. He could hardly contain himself as he showed us around.

"Now we'll enter the girl zone," he said, holding his nose. "Better give me a cootie shot before we go in."

I gave him a little pinch. "There you go," I said. "Though I don't know if it'll do any good, since a girl gave it to you."

"You're not a girl," he said. "You're a baby-sitter. And almost a grown-up."

"Thanks . . . I think," I said, laughing.

Buddy led us to a closed door and knocked loudly. "Anybody home?" he asked. "Can we come in?"

"Who's there?" called a voice from inside. It sounded like Lindsey to me.

"It's me, Buddy."

"And all of us baby-sitters," Kristy added.

"Come on in," said Lindsey, throwing the door open. "Welcome to our humble abode!"

The room was large and full of light. There were three beds: one each for Lindsey, Suzi, and Madeleine. It was decorated simply, with lots of primary colors. Madeleine's bedspread was yellow, Suzi's was green, and Lindsey's was red. Each of the girls had her own bureau and bookshelf, and there was a huge closet along one wall.

"Terrific room," said Abby.

"I love it," said Claudia.

"And we have a secret door!" whispered Madeleine.

Lindsey rolled her eyes. "Not too much of a secret anymore," she said with a rueful smile. "I think Mad's told every single person who's come through on the tour." She shrugged. "It's still neat," she said. "Want to see?" She showed us the secret hidey-hole built into the closet wall.

"Neat," said Kristy. "We'll do our best to forget about it, so it'll be a secret again."

"Now come see our room," said Buddy, tugging on my hand. "The boys' room *rules*!"

He led us into the room he'll be sharing with Taylor. It was another big, bright room, also decorated in primary colors. But the walls were already cluttered with posters of hockey stars, basketball players, and baseball heroes. The bureau tops were crammed with action figures, sports equipment, and assorted junk.

"Isn't it great?" asked Taylor, who was sitting on the floor, organizing a collection of Legos. Nicky Pike sat next to him, building a tower.

"It's perfect," I said, meaning it. It wasn't decorated to *my* taste, but I knew the boys would be as happy as clams in their new environment.

"Kids!" called Mrs. DeWitt from downstairs. "Time to open presents!"

"Yea!" yelled the kids. They ran out of their rooms, banging the doors and thundering down the stairs. We followed more sedately.

Many of the guests had brought housewarming presents (though we hadn't, since Mrs. DeWitt had specifically told us baby-sitters that our "presence" was our present), and they were piled high on the coffee table in the living room. Franklin, who's good at organizing things, made sure that each kid had a turn to rip into the wrapping paper.

The presents were awesome. There were posters and stuffed animals and stained-glass suncatchers for the windows. Dr. Johanssen gave the kids a huge easel with a blackboard on it for the playroom. The Kuhns' present was extra towels for the bathrooms, and the Pikes had chipped in for two beautiful rag rugs. Best of all, Eddie had made gorgeous carved-wood signs for each room, with all the kids' names on them.

"Excellent," said Buddy with satisfaction. He was sitting on the floor, surrounded by unwrapped presents and piles of discarded wrapping paper.

Presents over, everyone went back to eating, drinking, and talking (the adults), and running, shouting, and goofing around (the kids). At one point, Kristy and I headed into the kitchen to fetch some more bottles of soda. That's when I happened to look out the window.

"Hey, I thought everything was all done," I said. "What's that truck doing there?"

Kristy joined me at the window and took a look. "That's odd," she said.

"What's odd?" asked Buddy from behind us.

"That big truck parked out in the yard," I said.

Buddy shrugged. "I'll ask Eddie," he said, running off to find his favorite new pal.

In a few moments, he was back with Eddie. "See?" he asked.

"Would you look at that," said Eddie. "Guess I'll have to move that truck out of the yard. Can't leave trucks cluttering up the place, now, can I?" He reached into his pocket for the keys. "I may need some help backing out," he told Buddy. "How about if you round up all the kids and bring them outside."

I was beginning to think something was up. Eddie had a certain twinkle in his eye.

Buddy ran to find the other kids, and Eddie headed outside. Then, when everyone had gathered, he honked the horn three times — loudly — and backed up the truck. There, standing proudly in a spot that the truck had hidden, was the playhouse.

"Whoa!" yelled Buddy, flinging his arms into the air as he ran toward the house. "Check it out!"

He and the other kids converged on the playhouse. Eddie parked the truck in front of the house and came back to join them. In fact, everyone at the party piled out of the house to see what the noise was about.

The playhouse looked perfect. Somehow, Eddie and his crew had managed to take it apart, carry it outside the shed, and put it back together so you'd never know what had happened. They'd even put up the artwork and hung the curtains. The kids swarmed all over the house, commenting on everything and shouting with happiness. Eddie just stood and watched, wearing a satisfied smile.

Then I saw Suzi sidle up to him shyly. "Thanks, Eddie," she said with her best smile as she slipped her hand into his. You could see that for the Barrett and DeWitt kids life was perfect.

CHAPTER 14

"Aaaughh!" I let out a mock-horrified scream and pretended to tear out my hair. I was glaring at the huge pile of clothes that covered my bed. Why is it so hard sometimes to find something to wear? I mean, basically, clothes were invented for one purpose: to cover us up and keep us warm. (Okay, so that's two purposes. But you know what I mean.) So how did dressing for a party become so complex?

My blue velvet dress is pretty, but I'd be way too hot in it. My yellow-checked sundress is a big favorite of Logan's — and of mine — but it was starting to feel chilly in the evenings and my bare shoulders might freeze. Jeans were too informal. Ditto for overall shorts. But I didn't want to feel overdressed, either. Granny and Pop-Pop's surprise anniversary party was going to be a fun bash, not a stuffy affair.

I threw open the door of my closet one more time, hoping that the perfect piece of clothing might materialize in there since I'd last looked. "Beam me up one not-too-hot, not-too-cool, not-too-dressy, not-too-sloppy outfit, Scotty!" I giggled to myself.

I pulled out a floaty, flowered skirt and a short-sleeved white sweater. Logan says the skirt makes me look like a hippie, but I happen to like it. I held both items up in front of me and posed in front of the mirror. I didn't mind what I saw, so I tossed the skirt and sweater on top of the pile on my bed as a definite maybe.

It was Friday, a week after the addition-warming party at the Barrett-DeWitts'. Granny and Pop-Pop were back from their trip — Sharon and I had picked them up that morning — and their party was only hours away.

The day before, we'd spent the morning doing everything we could to make sure that their house would be welcoming and comfortable, even though both Jim and Eddie still had work to finish. We'd vacuumed and scrubbed and dusted and polished and made beds. The basement was almost completely dry by then, so we'd returned all the pieces of salvaged furniture to their proper places. In the afternoon, Esther had come by with a beautiful quilt she'd found at a craft show. It was a present for Granny to replace the one that had been ruined in the flood. With Esther's help we'd even done a little bit of weeding in the garden. And we'd managed to make the dug-up places in the yard — some for the plumbing and one for the "treasure" — look a little less raw.

Finally, we cut some flowers and arranged them in vases. Then we hung up a big, colorful "Welcome Home" banner that Dad and I had made on the computer. The place looked terrific.

"The place looks terrific!" That was the first thing Pop-Pop said as we pulled into the driveway. Granny didn't say a thing, but I could see from the smile on her face that she was happy to be home.

Both of them looked incredibly tan and rested. They'd had a great time on the cruise. On the way back from Manhattan, they couldn't stop talking about the delicious food, the islands they'd visited, the people they'd met, the helpful crew. It sounded as if they'd had the best vacation ever. Still, they said they felt ready to come home. I sensed that they were apprehensive about how the house would look. That's why I was happy to hear the relief in Pop-Pop's voice when he realized that the house was still in one piece.

Granny and Pop-Pop headed inside, while Sharon and I brought up the rear, carrying their luggage. "How about that!" said Pop-Pop when he saw the banner. "Isn't that something."

"And look at the lovely flowers, dear," said Granny. She turned to Sharon. "I can't thank you enough for all you've done."

Sharon smiled. "Mary Anne and her friends helped a lot," she said. "Why don't we take a look downstairs so you can see how things are coming along? I think I hear Jim and Eddie down there."

Pop-Pop led the way. I had the feeling he was holding his breath, waiting to see how bad the damage was. Jim Prentice met us at the bottom of the stairs.

"Welcome home," he said. "I hope you had a good trip."

"It was wonderful," said Granny.

"Can you show us around, tell us what you've been working on?" asked Pop-Pop, cutting to the heart of the matter.

"I'd be happy to," said Jim. "Let's see if Eddie can come along, too." He called for Eddie, who joined us and was introduced in turn. Then he and Jim took Granny and Pop-Pop on a tour of the rooms, showing them all the work that had been done so far and describing what still had to be finished. Sharon and I followed.

Pop-Pop listened carefully, nodding and saying, "Uh-huh" and "I see" as the men described the damage and the repairs. Granny was mostly concerned with the way things looked. "My goodness," she kept saying. "I thought it would be much worse." She loved the quilt Esther had brought over and thought the secondhand bureau we'd found was even nicer than the ruined one it had replaced.

The hardest part about being with Granny and Pop-Pop was remembering not to spoil the surprise. The party was going to be held at our house, but as far as Granny and Pop-Pop knew, they were just coming over for a quiet family dinner. Sharon had invited them, saying she knew they wouldn't feel like cooking on their first night back.

You'd think it would be easy to keep from mentioning the party. Not true. I was the first one to slip when Granny asked me what time Sharon wanted them to arrive. "She said around six, is that right?"

"No!" I said, a little too vehemently. "Six-*thirty*." If Granny and Pop-Pop showed up too early, they'd arrive at the same time as the guests, and there'd be no surprise.

Granny looked a little taken back. "Six-thirty's fine," she said, giving me an odd look.

"It's just — it's just that I need some time after my BSC meeting," I said lamely. "To, um, help Sharon with dinner."

Eddie was standing near me and Granny. He took advantage of the fact that her back was turned. He pointed at himself, then tapped his watch, then raised his eyebrows. "Six?" he mouthed. He was asking me what time he was supposed to arrive. (We'd invited the crews of workers. Even though Granny and Pop-Pop didn't know them, we figured they were practically part of the family by now, after all the time they'd put in at the house.)

I was nodding to Eddie when I noticed Pop-Pop, who had just come around the corner, staring at him. He must have thought that Eddie had lost his mind. Quickly, I changed my nod into a shrug as I exchanged bewildered glances with Pop-Pop. I tried to make my look project an "I have no idea what this guy is trying to say" kind of feeling.

Sharon almost slipped as well when she begged Pop-Pop not to wear "those awful Bermuda shorts" that night. He couldn't understand why it mattered what he wore, and he said he was tired of dressing for dinner every night on board the ship. But, fortunately, he let the matter slide, promising to make himself "presentable," if it mattered so much to his daughter.

Jim was the only one who kept it together, maintaining a professional attitude as he guided Pop-Pop through the basement, explaining every step of the repairs.

Anyway, we managed to make it through the morning without spilling the beans. After a quick lunch (we'd stocked their fridge with the basics), Sharon and I headed home to take care of some of the final details for that night. We finished decorating the house and checked in with the caterer and the florist. (Sharon had decided to hire professional help, since we'd been so busy working on Granny and Pop-Pop's house.)

At five-twenty, I headed over to Claudia's for our BSC meeting, bringing the music box with me. Since we'd been working on the mystery, we'd agreed to spend at least part of our meeting that afternoon discussing any clues that turned up.

Unfortunately, there wasn't much to discuss. The mystery at Granny and Pop-Pop's seemed to be over. Every avenue we'd followed had turned out to be a dead end. Jessi had checked into all the other owners of the house, but she hadn't turned up any interesting leads. Claudia's photography skills had failed her. And Mal's search of Stoneybrookites with the initials L. S. or H. I. W. hadn't come to anything.

"Play the music box one more time," Mal begged me. "I know it doesn't help us solve the mystery, but I like hearing the song."

I set the box in the middle of the room and opened the lid. The tinkling sounds poured out, echoing through the silence as we sat and listened and thought.

Well, most of us were thinking. Claudia was

comparing a regular Three Musketeers bar to a "lite" version. As she put it, she'd given up completely on the music box mystery and moved on to important scientific research.

I played the song again and again, thinking about the words that went with the music. I thought about L. S. and H. I. W. standing on opposite sides of the world, looking up at the stars and thinking of each other. I wondered if L. S. had gone out to look at the night sky as soon as darkness fell. I could almost picture her, searching for that first faint star.

"Whoa!" I said out loud, startling myself as well as everyone else in the room.

"What is it?" asked Kristy.

"I think I just figured something out," I said slowly. "I think I know what H. I. W. and L. S. stand for."

"You're kidding," said Abby.

"Think about it," I said. "What are the words of this song?" My friends looked at me as if I were nuts. But I began to sing "Twinkle, twinkle little star," and my friends began to join in. First Claudia, then Mal, then everyone chimed in on the next line. "How I wonder what you are."

"How I Wonder," I said. "I'm sure that's what H. I. W. stands for."

"What about L. S.?" asked Jessi.

"Little Star," said Stacey. "Little Star! That

has to be it!" She and I looked at each other, smiling. We knew we'd found the answer. Or at least part of it.

In case you're wondering, I finally settled on the flowery skirt with a silky blue blouse. I dressed quickly, then ran downstairs to ask Sharon if I could borrow a piece of her jewelry to dress up my outfit. She sent me to her room, saying I was welcome to go through her jewelry box. And that's where I found it. Another piece of the puzzle.

Nestled deep in the bottom of the box, in the midst of a tangle of necklaces, I found a silver bracelet.

A silver ID bracelet engraved with stars.

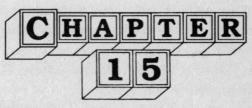

CHAPTER 15

"Oh, that old bracelet," said Sharon when I ran downstairs to show it to her. "I haven't seen that in ages." She took it from me and looked at it fondly.

"It was at the bottom of your jewelry box," I said. "Where did it come from, anyway?" I didn't have time to beat around the bush. Our guests were due to arrive any minute.

"As a matter of fact," said Sharon, "Granny gave it to me. On the night of my senior prom. I remember her saying something about how I should never forget my first love. I think she was sort of apologizing for the way she and Pop-Pop disapproved of Richard and were basically forcing us to break up." Sharon looked lost in memories.

I remembered when Dawn and I had found a rose pressed into Sharon's yearbook; a rose my father had given her on the night of their senior prom. How strange that my dad was actually someone's first love! And how amazing that he and Sharon ended up together after all this time. I don't think many people end up marrying their first love.

I felt myself drifting into a romantic cloud, but I pulled myself back. There were still some questions I had to have answered. I cleared my throat. "Sharon, do you know where Granny got this bracelet?" I asked.

Sharon came out of her daze. "You know, it's odd, but I don't know. It was something she'd owned for awhile, but I have no idea where it came from. I don't think she ever told me." She touched the bracelet one more time, tracing one of the stars engraved on it. "In any case, I certainly don't mind if you borrow it, and I don't think she would, either." Then she glanced at her watch. "Oh, no," she said with a groan. "People are going to be here any second, and I haven't even put the dip out yet."

"I'll help," I said. I fastened the bracelet onto my wrist. I still had so many questions about it. How did Granny come to own it? Had Lydia — who *must* be Little Star — given it to her for some reason? Whatever happened to How I Wonder? What did Granny know about the story of their romance? My mind was whirling.

"Oh, there's the phone," said Sharon. "I'll grab it, if you can just start setting out the dip and chips." She gave my shoulder a quick squeeze. "You look wonderful, Mary Anne. And thanks for your help. I don't know what I'd do without you."

She dashed off toward the phone, and I dashed off toward the kitchen. For the moment, I forgot about the bracelet and the questions it had raised.

I set out the dip and chips, and the sodas and the cups, and the paper plates and napkins. I unwrapped the food the caterers had dropped off and set it out as well, making sure that there were enough large serving spoons handy. The food looked terrific. Sharon had ordered all kinds of yummy things such as shish kebab and chicken teriyaki and huge platters of vegetables for dipping. Even though Sharon's a vegetarian and into eating healthily, she knows what most people are looking for at a party.

Logan was one of the first guests to arrive. "You look really pretty," he said, kissing me. Then he turned his attention to the food. (Typical boy.) I had to stop him from digging right in.

"We can't eat until Granny and Pop-Pop arrive!" I said.

Logan looked so disappointed that I relented. "Okay, go ahead and have some chicken. Nobody will ever know."

He kissed me again, grabbed a piece of chicken, and took off to see who else was arriving.

The doorbell began ringing almost continuously as people piled into the house. Everybody was in good spirits, trying to top each other's tales of how they'd nearly messed up the surprise. Esther had spoken to Granny on the phone and ended the conversation by saying, "See you tonight!" She'd had to think fast to cover her mistake, but Granny hadn't seemed to notice.

"I'll bet she already knows about the party," said Hank the Grump. "You can't put one over on Gracie."

"I wouldn't be so sure," said Eddie, who'd overheard Hank's comment. "The last thing I heard her say as I was leaving this afternoon was that she was looking forward to a nice, quiet evening with the family tonight." He grinned at me and winked. "So, as hard as we all tried to blow it, I think they'll still be surprised."

Guess what? They were. At least, as far I could tell. When they arrived, Sharon and Dad and I chatted with them for a few moments in the front hall. Then we casually wandered into the living room — where all their nearest and dearest friends happened to be sitting around. (Sharon and I had decided that the jumping-out-of-hiding-places-and-yelling type of surprise might be a little much for her parents, so we'd opted for a lower-key approach.)

"What – ?" said Granny as she slowly took in the scene.

"Hey," said Pop-Pop when he saw two of his best friends from his former job. "What's going on here?"

"A party," said Sharon, walking toward her parents and taking each of them by the hand. "To celebrate a couple whose marriage is a model for all of us. And to wish you many more years of happiness!"

The guests applauded. Granny and Pop-Pop stood in the middle of the room, looking just a tiny bit overcome.

Dad came to the rescue. "And now, how about some dinner?" he asked. "After all, that's what we invited you here for." He offered his arm to Granny, and Sharon took Pop-Pop's arm. "Shall we?" asked Dad, sweeping Granny toward the long table in the dining room, which was piled high with food.

That was enough to break the ice. Soon the table was surrounded by people loading up plates, filling glasses, and grabbing hunks of garlic bread. Then everyone moved into the living room and began to eat, balancing plates on their knees.

Logan and I waited until the rush was over.

Then we approached the table together and filled up a huge plate of food to share. We took our feast to a quiet spot in a corner of the living room. It didn't stay quiet for long, since all my BSC friends soon joined us, but still, it was nice to share a meal with Logan.

I was just finishing my last meatball when Granny poked her head around the corner. "Mary Anne," she said, "do you suppose you could help me find something in the kitchen? I don't want to bother Sharon right now."

"Sure," I said, jumping up. I followed her into the kitchen, and she told me that she was looking for some antacids for Pop-Pop.

"I'm afraid he has a little indigestion," she confessed. "All that rich food on the ship, and now this wonderful party."

I smiled. "Maybe these will make him feel better," I said, reaching into the cabinet over the sink for the antacid tablets. "So, are you enjoying the party?"

"Oh, yes," she said. "It's lovely to see all our friends, especially after being away. It was so thoughtful of Sharon to arrange this, and so nice of you to help her out."

"I was glad to do it," I said.

"Your young man," Granny said. "What is his name again?"

I blushed a little. It was funny to hear Logan

referred to as my "young man." "Logan," I said. "Logan Bruno."

"Well, he seems very nice," she said. "And you two make an adorable couple." She sighed. "There's nothing like a first love. Savor it, my dear. You'll always remember him, no matter what your future brings." She had a faraway look in her eyes, and she wore a faint smile.

"Granny," I said impulsively, "do you know anything about this bracelet?" I held up my wrist. Granny gave a little gasp. "I have a feeling it belonged to a girl who used to live in your house," I said. "A girl named Lydia? I think her boyfriend gave it to her. They called each other Little Star and How I Wonder. Do you remember writing to your cousin June about their romance?"

I'd thought she'd be surprised at how much I knew, but Granny still hadn't spoken. In fact, she hadn't taken her eyes off the bracelet.

"Granny?" I asked, suddenly concerned. "Are you feeling all right?"

"I'm fine," she said. She reached out and touched one of the stars on the bracelet. "And I do, indeed, remember Lydia and her boyfriend," she said. "But this bracelet didn't belong to her. It belonged to me. I was Little Star."

"You?" I gasped.

She nodded. "That's what Frank called me. And I called him How I Wonder. Silly names, but that's how young lovers are." She still had that faraway look in her eyes.

"Frank?" I asked, shaking my head as if to clear it. I'd grown used to thinking of the boy in the picture — and the sailor in my dreams — as Johnny, since I'd been so sure that he was Lydia's boyfriend. Granny was turning everything upside down.

"That was his name," she said. "I met him at the ice-cream shop. He was my first true love. He gave me the most beautiful music box in the world. Then he went off to war and was killed."

Killed? How awful. I couldn't even speak. I reached out and hugged Granny. "The music box really is beautiful," I mumbled into her shoulder.

"So you opened it despite the horrible warning?" asked Granny. I stood back from her and nodded. She laughed. "I wrote that when I was younger, to keep out snoops," she said. I suddenly remembered that the handwriting in young Grace's letters had looked somehow familiar. It must have reminded me of the handwriting on the wrapper. "You know, I never told *anyone* about Frank. He's my secret. I kept that box, of course, but always hidden. When Pop-Pop and I moved to that house and I saw that cubbyhole, I tucked the box away there and never told a soul."

"I won't tell anyone, either," I promised.

"Thank you," she said, looking at me very seriously, then reaching out to hug me again. "I'd like you to have the music box, Mary Anne," she said. "It's yours, as long as you keep my secret."

"My lips are sealed," I replied, thinking that I'd have to come up with some story to satisfy my friends' curiosity about the mystery of L. S. and H. I. W. "And I'll treasure the music box forever."

Granny and I talked for a little while longer in the kitchen that night, about first loves and lost loves and secret loves. Then we realized we'd better rejoin the party. "Just tell me one more thing," I asked her. "Whatever happened to Johnny and Lydia?"

Granny laughed. "Them? Well, they eloped. Oh, my, it was so romantic and thrilling. But you know what's funny? They're still married, all these years later, and they're the most boring old couple you'd ever want to meet!"

Back in the midst of the party a few minutes later, I watched Granny dance around the room in Pop-Pop's arms. And when I saw the way she looked into his eyes, I knew for sure that even though Frank may have been Granny's first love, Pop-Pop was the love of her life.

I never did tell Granny about the way I'd dreamed of Frank. I guess I was afraid it might upset her. But I did have one last dream about my sailor boy, the night after the party. Once again, I saw him from a distance, and I sensed a question in those beautiful blue eyes of his. But this time, he was able to talk to me, and I finally found out what the question was. "How is she?" he asked me. "How is my Grace, my Little Star?"

I told him she was fine, happy and healthy. He seemed satisfied. His eyes lost that sad look. And after that, I never dreamed about him again. But every now and then I look at the music box sitting on my bureau, and I think about first love, and I sigh.

L. GODWIN

Ann M. Martin

About the Author

ANN MATTHEWS MARTIN was born on August 12, 1955. She grew up in Princeton, NJ, with her parents and her younger sister, Jane.

Although Ann used to be a teacher and then an editor of children's books, she's now a full-time writer. She gets the ideas for her books from many different places. Some are based on personal experiences. Others are based on childhood memories and feelings. Many are written about contemporary problems or events.

All of Ann's characters, even the members of the Baby-sitters Club, are made up. (So is Stoneybrook.) But many of her characters are based on real people. Sometimes Ann names her characters after people she knows, other times she chooses names she likes.

In addition to the Baby-sitters Club books, Ann Martin has written many other books for children. Her favorite is *Ten Kids, No Pets* because she loves big families and she loves animals. Her favorite Baby-sitters Club book is *Kristy's Big Day*. (By the way, Kristy is her favorite baby-sitter!)

Ann M. Martin now lives in New York with her cats, Gussie and Woody. Her hobbies are reading, sewing, and needlework — especially making clothes for children.

Look for Mystery #32

Claudia and the Mystery in the Painting

I heard a sickening thud as I rounded the corner at the bottom of the staircase. The painting had been leaning against the newel post and when I flew by it, I knocked it over. Slowly, I picked it up and turned it over, hoping I hadn't caused any irreparable damage. A few flakes of paint drifted off as I turned it right side up, but otherwise it seemed okay.

A shadow fell over me, and I expected to see Ms. Madden when I looked up. Instead, I saw Mr. Cook, frowning as usual.

"What have you done now?" he asked in his deep voice.

"I was looking for this painting and when I walked by," I cleared my throat, "it fell over."

He grabbed the painting out of my hands. "Where did you find this? This could be very valuable," he said. "My wife must be out of her mind to let a bunch of kids handle these things." He turned his back on me and started up the steps.

"I wanted to check one thing," I said, reaching out.

"No one but an appraiser is going to check anything," said Mr. Cook. "I'm not sure you understand how valuable some of Rebecca's grandmother's things may be," he added in a little softer tone. "We appreciate your help with Jimmy and with all the sorting, but there are some things that you need to leave to those who know something about art and antiques."

Mr. Cook held the painting carefully, as if it might break, as he climbed the stairs. I expected to see him turn toward the studio, but he disappeared into a bedroom, shutting the door firmly behind him.

Did he suspect the painting was a Madden too?

Read all the books
about **Mary Anne**
in the Baby-sitters Club series
by Ann M. Martin

THE BABY-SITTERS CLUB®

by Ann M. Martin

Collect and read these exciting BSC Super Specials, Mysteries, and Super Mysteries along with your favorite Baby-sitters Club books!

BSC Super Specials

❏ BBK44240-6	Baby-sitters on Board! Super Special #1	$3.95
❏ BBK44239-2	Baby-sitters' Summer Vacation Super Special #2	$3.95
❏ BBK43973-1	Baby-sitters' Winter Vacation Super Special #3	$3.95
❏ BBK42493-9	Baby-sitters' Island Adventure Super Special #4	$3.95
❏ BBK43575-2	California Girls! Super Special #5	$3.95
❏ BBK43576-0	New York, New York! Super Special #6	$4.50
❏ BBK44963-X	Snowbound! Super Special #7	$3.95
❏ BBK44962-X	Baby-sitters at Shadow Lake Super Special #8	$3.95
❏ BBK45661-X	Starring The Baby-sitters Club! Super Special #9	$3.95
❏ BBK45674-1	Sea City, Here We Come! Super Special #10	$3.95
❏ BBK47015-9	The Baby-sitters Remember Super Special #11	$3.95
❏ BBK48308-0	Here Come the Bridesmaids! Super Special #12	$3.95
❏ BBK22883-8	Aloha, Baby-sitters! Super Special #13	$4.50

BSC Mysteries

❏ BAI44084-5	#1 Stacey and the Missing Ring	$3.50
❏ BAI44085-3	#2 Beware Dawn!	$3.50
❏ BAI44799-8	#3 Mallory and the Ghost Cat	$3.50
❏ BAI44800-5	#4 Kristy and the Missing Child	$3.50
❏ BAI44801-3	#5 Mary Anne and the Secret in the Attic	$3.50
❏ BAI44961-3	#6 The Mystery at Claudia's House	$3.50
❏ BAI44960-5	#7 Dawn and the Disappearing Dogs	$3.50
❏ BAI44959-1	#8 Jessi and the Jewel Thieves	$3.50
❏ BAI44958-3	#9 Kristy and the Haunted Mansion	$3.50
❏ BAI45696-2	#10 Stacey and the Mystery Money	$3.50
❏ BAI47049-3	#11 Claudia and the Mystery at the Museum	$3.50

More titles ➡

The Baby-sitters Club books continued...

Available wherever you buy books...or use this order form.

Scholastic Inc., P.O. Box 7502, 2931 East McCarty Street, Jefferson City, MO 65102-7502

Please send me the books I have checked above. I am enclosing $ _____
(please add $2.00 to cover shipping and handling). Send check or money order
— no cash or C.O.D.s please.

Name_____Birthdate_____

Address _____

City_____State/Zip_____

Please allow four to six weeks for delivery. Offer good in the U.S. only. Sorry, mail orders are not
available to residents of Canada. Prices subject to change.

BSCM1196